OUR STORIES CONTINUE
VOLUME 1

A SHORT STORY ANTHOLOGY BY
SAPPHIRE BOOKS AUTHORS

OUR STORIES CONTINUE VOLUME 1

A SHORT STORY ANTHOLOGY BY SAPPHIRE BOOKS AUTHORS

EDITED BY ELIZABETH M. HODGE

SAPPHIRE BOOKS

SALINAS, CALIFORNIA

Sapphire Books Publishing, LLC
P.O. Box 8142
Salinas, CA 93912
www.sapphirebooks.com

Printed in the United States of America
First Edition – November 2016

This and other Sapphire Books titles can be found at
www.sapphirebooks.com

This soul, or life within us, by no means agrees with the life outside us. If one has the courage to ask her what she thinks, she is always saying the very opposite to what other people say.

Virginia Woolf

Introduction

Sapphire Books publishes works by tremendously gifted authors who write across the genre spectrum. From speculative fiction, mystery, romance and erotica, science fiction, poetry and beyond, Sapphire Books makes a commitment to providing lesbian fiction readers with an abundance of books for a variety of tastes. *Sapphire Books: Our Stories Continue: Volume 1,* the first in a series of short story anthologies designed to showcase the talent of Sapphire authors. A few stories, such as Linda North's *Bedtime for Kedru Kits,* and Sheila Powell and Liz McMullen's *Mercy Lost* focus on characters from bestselling novels. Other entries give snippets of new works in progress or simply a glimpse into the imagination, sense of humor, depth of emotion, and, perhaps, romantic disposition of the author. More romance abounds throughout the book than any other theme, since Sapphire authors (the Sapphire Sisters) are a passionate group of women, who love to *"LOVE"* just as much as they enjoy writing!

Table of Contents

Survivor

By Kim Pritekel

Denny wished she could shut out the horrible screaming of the plane as it cut through the whipping air, the plane once more tilting nose-down. She could feel the plastic covering on the armrest beginning to give way beneath her iron grip. Regardless, there was no way she was releasing it. The plane righted itself again then Denny was jostled like never before.

There was a loud bang as something hit them from underneath, and the sound of screeching metal seemed to last forever. When it stopped, there was a horrible rushing sound.

Oh, Jesus...

There was a second jolt, with a louder bang coming from much closer beneath them. Suddenly there was an amazing amount of light bleeding through the cabin, followed by a deafening scream, like the day itself was wailing its anger, pain, and regret.

"They're gone!" Denny yelled, shooting up in bed, the sheet falling to gather at her waist. "They're gone!"

"Denny?"

Hand to her heaving chest, Denny glanced over to see Rachel staring at her from over her shoulder as she lay on her side, back to Denny. "Are you okay?"

Denny nodded, running her hands through long, dark hair. "Yeah. Go back to sleep. Sorry I woke you."

Rachel got settled again and Denny considered joining her, but knew that sleep wouldn't be coming back anytime soon. Glancing at the bedside clock, she saw that it was nearly five-thirty in the morning, and she'd be getting up in two hours, anyway.

As quietly as she could, Denny climbed out of bed and padded to the bathroom in the hall, avoiding the master bath so as not to disturb Rachel any further than she already had.

Closing the door before she turned on the light, Denny studied her reflection. Tired, haunted blue eyes looked back at her. Too many nightmare-filled nights lately making them red and puffy.

"I can't go through this again," she whispered to her non-responding reflection. Blowing out a breath, she decided to get ready and head to the café early.

❧ ❧ ❧ ❧

Before the dubious honor of becoming a member of the island six, Denny had given her time, love and passion to DiRisio's in Buffalo, NY, the coffee shop she'd owned before the plane crash that changed her life forever and that brought Rachel Holt into her life and heart.

Even though Hannah, Denny's partner before she took the flight to Italy, had sold the coffee shop, thinking Denny was dead, Denny never forgot about how much she loved the extremely successful business she'd built from the ground up, the food industry coming very natural to her. So, three years ago, she and Rachel had decided it was time for Denny's dream to be reborn, and so the birth of the I Six Café came to fruition. The other four survivors had gone in with them, each an equal investor scattered all over the country, trusting in Denny to turn a profit and make them all proud. She'd done just that. The youngest of the survivors – only seventeen at the time of the accident – Mia told them she wanted a more personal, hands-on experience, so she'd gone to culinary school and then she and then-boyfriend, Paul had picked up stakes and moved across the country to Oregon. Her skills and talent had turned the I Six into the most popular eatery in the entire county.

She searched through her key ring until she found the right key and let herself in through the kitchen door at the back of the building, which sat thirty-two patrons. As she entered the dark building, she thought about Rachel back home. Denny hadn't awoken her up before she'd left but had simply sent her a text before she'd pulled out of the garage, knowing that Rachel would get it when she woke up. She felt guilty, as she knew she'd been holding back from her partner of almost six years, but she just couldn't shake the returning trauma that had been haunting her now for months. She knew what it was and why it was, but still, she couldn't shake it.

Walking through the building, Denny flicked on lights as she went, eyeing the job her closing crew did the night before. Though Denny was a nice person and a great boss, she had extremely high standards when it came to her business and anyone who didn't follow those well-laid out standards didn't last long as an I Six employee.

Satisfied with the condition of the restaurant,

Denny made her way back to the kitchen and donned her apron as she began to prep for the day. This was usually work that Mia would do first thing, but this morning, Denny needed something to keep her mind and hands busy. She hoped that when Mia's husband Paul dropped her off, he'd have little Vincent, Mia and Paul's eighteen-month-old son and the second love of Denny's life.

She smiled as she thought about the toddler. She and Rachel often babysat for the young, newlywed couple. After all, they'd left everything behind for a new start at the café, even Mia's beloved mother, Gloria. Even still, what Mia didn't know was, Gloria had spoken to Denny about a waitressing job at I Six. She certainly had the experience, and she wanted to be close to her daughter and grandson.

As Denny continued chopping up vegetables for Mia's menu, she felt confusion and anger. She had the kind of life she'd always dreamed of, a fantasy to anyone else. She had a second chance at life with a second successful business, she was married to the love of her life and was surrounded by incredible people that she shared a deep and profound bond with.

But now, as the seven year anniversary of the crash loomed, she felt a panic inside her chest and flutter in her heart, almost as though that plane were going down all over again. Every time she looked at Rachel, she was reminded of what she'd lost and what she'd endured. Every time she looked into those beautiful green eyes that had captured her years before on the back cover of a book, she felt like she couldn't breathe. Denny felt like she was reliving the fear and panic all over again, every single moment in the waking day and the sleeping night.

Denny was surprised when she heard Paul's truck pull up to the building, not realizing it was as late as it was. Denny grabbed the towel that had been slung over her shoulder and wiped her hands as she waited for her chef's entrance. To her delight, Mia was followed by Paul and Vincent.

"Gimmie!" she exclaimed, opening her arms for the toddler who was already reaching for her. She rained kisses all over the giggling boy's face before she gave him a hearty squeeze. "I'm kidnapping him."

"Please?" Paul teased, running a hand through short, sandy blonde hair. "He's teething and oh boy, don't we know it."

"Are you Mr. Grumpy Pants?" Denny asked the child, holding him up to her eye-level. She gave him one more kiss before handing him back to his father. "Are we still keeping him Friday night?"

"If that's okay," Paul said, placing a quick kiss on Mia's lips. "See you later."

The two women left alone, Denny walked back to her chopped veggies, sorting the pieces into the correct containers to be put into the walk-in.

"Wow!" Mia said, gazing at Denny's handiwork. "What time did you get in?"

"Early,"

Mia rolled her eyes. "Clearly. You chopped up the entire produce section at Whole Foods."

Denny grinned, grunting as she grabbed a heavy container of meat from a shelf in the walk-in. "Couldn't sleep." She set it down, checking the date label to make sure she had the right one.

"Nightmares again?"

Denny stopped what she was doing at the quiet words. She took a moment then spared a glance at her young friend. Without a word, she nodded before pulling the lid off the meat container. "Yeah. All damn night."

"You should get in and talk to someone, Denny. This time of year always hits you pretty hard," Mia suggested as she washed her hands.

Denny let out a heavy sigh. "Yeah."

Later that afternoon Denny sat in her office going over some invoices when a knock sounded on the closed door. "It's open!" she called, comparing the figures on an invoice to those on the budget spreadsheet on her computer screen. The door opened and someone stepped in. "Hang on one sec," she murmured, not wanting to lose her place.

"Sweets, this isn't how you treat a guest."

Denny's head flew up and her mouth fell open. "Dean!" Denny pushed back from the desk and flew around it to be engulfed in a strong embrace. After a long moment she pulled back to look him over. He was tan and well-dressed with his ever-present loafers and of course, always at the crown of style, his hair short and perfect.

"You look gorgeous," she said giving him another hug before leaning back on the edge of her desk and crossing her arms over her chest. "What are you doing here?"

"Well," he said, leaning a shoulder against the wall in the tiny office. "I came by to see how things are going around here."

"That's new," Denny quipped, moving back to her chair and indicating he should sit in the one across from her, which he did. "Normally I just get a demanding text, 'Where's my check?'"

Dean grinned and crossed one leg over the other,

running his fingers down the sharp seam of his slacks. "Well, I figured I'd shake things up. You know, make you sweat with the boss in town."

Denny smirked. "The boss my ass."

"I was in Portland for some case research so I figured I'd pop on over here and say hi. This place looks amazing, Denny. There isn't an empty seat out there," he added, hitching his thumb towards the office door that he closed before sitting down.

"Thank you," Denny said, filled with pride. She was proud of what they'd accomplished.

"Buuuuuut, little Mia says lately your happy ass is in here ridiculously early and then leaves ridiculously late." He held Denny's gaze for a long moment. "What's going on, Den?"

Denny looked away. She grabbed a pen from the desktop and twisted it between her fingers. At the sound of her name she gave him a side glance. "Did she call you?"

Dean shook his head and flopped an arm over the back of the chair. "When Rachel finished her latest book tour in Boston last month, she met Will and I for dinner."

Denny looked down again, unable to see the love and slight accusation in his eyes.

"The nightmares back?"

"Yup." Denny tossed the pen back to the desk, frustrated and feeling cornered. "You'd think after three and a half years of therapy I'd be over it."

"None of us will ever be over it, Denny. A thousand years of therapy couldn't make that happen."

"Then why can't I let it go?"

"Because it's part of you now, sweetheart. It's part of us all. You're not going to lose Rachel, Denny.

She's not going anywhere, your business isn't going anywhere and neither is the most important person in your life – me!"

Denny threw her head back and laughed, and it felt damn good.

"Listen," Dean said, pushing up from the chair and perching on the edge of her desk. "Rachel is the best thing that's ever happened to you and you're the best thing that's ever happened to her. She's confused and she's scared, Denny. You can't keep pushing her away. Let her in."

Denny ran her hands through her hair and let out a heavy sigh. "I know you're right."

"When's the last time you gave her a good pokey poke?" Dean asked, an eye brow raised.

"Um, isn't that what Will gives you, Mr. Queer As Folk?"

Dean grinned. "I'll take that as a compliment, and of course, every night. And, every morning, come to think of it."

Denny rolled her eyes. "You're such a pig. And, frankly, nothing is quite right at home," she admitted, though she could hardly look at her friend and business partner. "And, the worst part is, I absolutely know it's my fault." She pushed up from her chair and walked the couple feet to where Dean still perched on her desk. She squeezed his shoulder. "Come on. Let's get you some of Mia's famous lasagna. Nonna Lisbeth's recipe."

⚛ ⚛ ⚛ ⚛

Rachel sat behind the desk in her home office, the newest cover for her upcoming book, *Blinded* on the screen of her laptop, awaiting her approval. She couldn't focus, instead her mind was on her deeply troubled heart. Again she saw Denny's text to her that morning – like so many others lately.

Went in early. See you later.

No good morning, no I love you, nothing. The text had been as distant and removed as Denny's behavior the last few months, especially the past few weeks. She'd been fighting the most awful thoughts, thoughts that she knew spanned back to her ex-husband, Matt, and his unfaithful ways. She knew in her heart that Denny could not, *would* not cheat. But still…

"Hey."

Rachel nearly jumped out of her seat at the sudden sound of the voice of the very woman she'd just been contemplating. She looked up at see Denny leaning against the open doorway to the home office. She was casual in well-fitted jeans, as was her habit, and a t-shirt denoting the name and logo of their café.

"Hi." Rachel's surprise quickly passed, replaced by her hurt. "I got your text," she said, the words edged with bitterness. "I didn't expect you home before dinner, or perhaps even before bed."

Denny looked down at her shoes, the toe of one tapping the hardwood flooring beneath it. "I brought you home some of Mia's lasagna. I know you love it," she said, looking up to meet Rachel's hard gaze. "Wasn't sure if you'd had lunch or not."

Rachel contemplated the offer and for a moment, she wanted to be a bitch with a snarky remark, but decided against it. Rather than speaking, she pushed back from the desk and walked by Denny and towards the kitchen. She could hear Denny's footsteps behind her.

"Busy day today," Denny said, grabbing a plate from the cabinet.

"Good," Rachel responded, removing the wrapped food – still hot – from the plastic bag and foil it had been placed in to transport it home. "Thank you," she said quietly, accepting the plate Denny handed her. "I think the addition of Mia's cooking was really a smart idea." She gave Denny as much of a smile as she could muster. "Too bad she couldn't cook like that on the island, huh?"

Denny smirked, pouring two glasses of iced tea. "Very true."

The two fell silent as Rachel sucked a bit of marinara off her thumb as she grabbed a fork out of the drawer and carried her lunch to the table in the small eating nook, the formal dining set only used when they had family over or entertained.

Rachel put a bite in her mouth and studied her wife, noting the diamond-inlaid band in stark contrast to the tanned flesh of Denny's left ring finger. "So," she said, sending her gaze back to her plate. "Why are you home early? Or, are you heading back in after you finish your tea?"

Denny shook her head, taking a sip from the very tea Rachel mentioned. "No. It occurred to me that we hired a G.M. for a reason." She met Rachel's troubled gaze. "I wanted to come home to be with you. Is that okay? Or, are you editing or –"

"We finished edits two weeks ago, Denny," Rachel spat before slamming her fork down and shoving her chair away from the table. "What the hell is going on?" she demanded, her patience finally lost and frustration exploding. "Please tell me when exactly it was that I went to sleep and woke up with someone I barely know and recognize? Because I gotta tell you, Denny, I have no idea who you are right now. I have no idea what you want, what makes you tick, what you need…" She sent a beseeching look Denny's way. When there was nothing forthcoming she continued. "You're antsy and restless most the time and the rest of the time you're not even here!" She slammed her hands flat on the table, leaning on them as her eyes bored into Denny's. "I have to ask you something I never thought I'd have to ask again, and certainly not to you." She swallowed, her heart pounding and stomach threatening to rebel.

"Alright," Denny said softly.

"Denny, is there someone else?" Rachel was barely able to ask the question above a whisper.

"Yes," Denny said, the tiniest twinkle in her eyes. "He's about two and a half feet tall and has the longest eyelashes on the planet."

Rachel obviously saw Denny's attempt at humor but something inside her broke and the tears came in earnest. She'd been holding it in for far too many weeks, trying to give Denny her space to get through what was clearly eating her alive.

"Hey," Denny cooed, pushing away from the table and wrapping her arms around Rachel, who tried to push her away, but finally gave in. "I'm sorry," Denny whispered into Rachel's ear. "I'm so sorry."

"I don't know what to do," Rachel cried, clawing at Denny's shirt in desperation to have her as close as possible. "What did I do? What *can* I do?" She pulled away just enough to look up into Denny's eyes. "Please, Denny. Let me in. Talk to me!"

"Okay," Denny whispered, pulling Rachel's head back against her shoulder. "Okay."

Rachel felt herself calming and immediately getting lost in Denny's arms and in her warmth as they gently began to sway together. She tightened her hold as her eyes slid closed.

"There's nobody else, baby," Denny murmured into her hair. "Never. As a little birdie named Dean reminded me today, you're the best thing that's ever happened to me."

"Dean? Our Dean?" Rachel asked, her words slightly muffled into Denny's shirt.

"Is there any other?" Denny chuckled. "Fact is, I'm so terrified of losing you, the way Michael lost Melissa. I know he's married to Patrice now, but seeing what he went through." Rachel was squeezed tighter against her. "I couldn't survive it."

Rachel pulled away and brought her hands up to cup Denny's face, Denny's eyes welling. "Oh, baby," she whispered, slowly shaking her head. "I'm not going anywhere, Denny. Pushing me away isn't going to make it any easier." She ran a thumb under one of Denny's eyes as a tear began to escape. "Baby, please don't cry." She leaned up and placed a lingering kiss on soft lips.

"It's coming up on seven years," Denny said, her voice hoarse. "I've been reliving the horror of the crash every night."

"I know. I know. Me, too. But Denny," Rachel said gently, stroking a soft cheek with the backs of her fingers. "I don't see you as a symbol of the horror, but the light in the darkness, my beacon. You're my hope, my love and my life." Rachel's eyes slid closed at the kiss she received, just the touch of softness against softness for a long moment. She felt her world right itself in that moment.

"Rachel," Denny murmured against her lips, the

need in her voice striking Rachel's heart and beyond.

"I'm here, baby," Rachel responded,

"Rachel," Denny said again, her kiss now deep and demanding.

Rachel's arms slid up around Denny's neck and pulled them closer together as she found herself pushed up against the fridge, Denny's warmth pressed against her. She needed this, needed to feel the love that she knew was between them, a love that was sharp and intense and had gotten them through a year and a half on that island. She relished Denny's moan as she cupped her denim-clad behind, pulling her as close as possible.

Suddenly, Denny's kiss slowed then stopped as she rested her forehead against Rachel's. Rachel closed her eyes and absorbed the closeness. When Denny pulled away and looked at her, Rachel nearly cried, though tears of a new sort this time. In the oceanic depths of Denny's eyes, she saw the Denny she loved, the Denny she fell in love with so quickly and passionately. She reached up and cupped her beautiful face and leaned up to place a soft kiss upon her lips.

Without a word, Rachel took Denny's hand in her own and led her back through the house to their bedroom. Once there, she stopped them at the side of the bed and turned Denny to face her. She ran her hands up a flat, cotton-clad tummy before she cupped Denny's breasts, earning a soft sigh in return. They shared a lingering kiss that began a slow burn, Denny flicking Rachel's bottom lip with her tongue, asking for entry, which was immediately granted.

As the kiss continued, Rachel ran her hands back down Denny's torso to the hem of her shirt and tugged it upwards, bearing the smooth tanned flesh of

Denny's stomach, satin-clad breasts and upper chest. She sighed in appreciation into the kiss as she let the t-shirt fall to the floor at their feet. She left Denny's mouth and began to kiss and nip at her neck, the taller woman's head falling to the side.

"Rachel," Denny whispered.

Rachel hummed into her task as her fingers found the clasp at Denny's back, easily unsnapping it so the satin bra would come loose, the straps falling down Denny's arms to catch at the bend of her arms. Within a moment, that too, hit the floor. Rachel buried her face in the creamy flesh of Denny's breasts, her hands resting at her sides before her fingernails trailed down around to her back, causing a slight shudder through Denny's body. She laid a trail of kisses along Denny's collarbones and down between her breasts before she reached down and unfastened her jeans, slipping her hands inside to push down the denim over a shapely behind and strong thighs.

Standing before her in panties, Rachel took in the glorious woman before her. She ran her hands down smooth arms before she met Denny's hooded gaze. It had been far too long since they'd made love and even longer since she'd felt what she saw in those gorgeous blue eyes in that moment.

Taking a step back, Rachel never left Denny's gaze as she undressed, taking her time, just how she knew Denny like it. Naked, she took the couple steps back to her love and finished undressing her, red satin panties joining their pile of clothing. Rachel took Denny's hand once again and led her the couple steps to the bed, using her free hand to swipe throw pillows off the bed, their cat, Cara glaring at them before jumping down from the bed just in time before the comforter, blanket and sheet was tugged to the end of the bed.

Rachel pulled Denny down atop her, moaning at the feel of their warm nakedness coming together. She loved Denny's weight on top of her, the feeling reminding her that Denny would always protect her, always love her and always be with her. She initiated what was meant to be a slow, sensual kiss, but it didn't take long before passion overtook them and it became deep and wet.

Rachel moaned as Denny left her mouth, her own exploring over Rachel's neck and upper chest. Green eyes closed when a hard nipple was engulfed in the warm wetness of Denny's mouth. Rachel buried her hands in thick dark hair, pulling Denny harder against her breast. Her soft moans turned into outright guttural groans as Denny insinuated a thigh between Rachel's legs, pressing against the wet heat that immediately painted smooth flesh.

As Denny began to move against Rachel's need, the blonde tugged at her, Denny's mouth returning to her own. Their kiss was deep and filled with mutual need. It didn't take long for Rachel to fall over the edge, pulling away from the kiss as she cried out. Nowhere near satiated, as she felt the need to claim Denny, she used near-animalistic strength to push Denny off of her and to her back. She gave the startled blue eyes a sexy little grin as she climbed on top of the taller woman, making her intentions quite clear as her hand immediately found the volcano between Denny's thighs.

"This belongs to me," she murmured against Denny's lips as she cupped her, Denny's groan long and deep, sending renewed wetness between Rachel's own thighs.

Rachel took Denny in a hard kiss as her fingers pushed through swollen folds, easily finding a hard, slick clit. She used two fingers to rub in a slow circle, refusing to hasten her speed, even as Denny's whimpers became desperate. Rachel forced herself to remain in control, almost feeling a need to punish Denny, to let her know that it was not okay to shut down and leave Rachel behind ever again. Denny seemed to get the idea as she cried out loud and long as she came, her need covering Rachel's fingers.

The intensity of her sudden emotion and hurt sated, Rachel lay next to Denny and brought up a hand to cup her left breast as she initiated a slow and loving kiss, teasing Denny's lips with her own. She deepened the kiss slightly when she felt Denny's hand bury itself in her hair, which cascaded down around them, a golden curtain to close the world in to only the two of them.

Rachel brushed her thumb over a hard nipple before taking it between two fingers, gently twisting and tugging on it before she brought her mouth to it. She heard Denny's contented sigh as she batted at the rigid flesh with her tongue, moaning into her task. She dipped two fingers into Denny's wetness then painted the flesh around the nipple with it, her tongue following in a fiery trail. She loved the taste of Denny's passion, loved how Denny's body had been to her touch since as early as their days on the island. She wanted more.

Moving between spreading legs, Rachel got herself settled and comfortable on her belly, her arms wrapping around strong thighs, which she forced fully open, her hands splayed out on Denny's stomach. She smiled when a larger hand slipped over one of hers. Their eyes met briefly before Rachel turned her focus fully on the feast before her. Her mouth watered as she closed her eyes at the first swipe of her tongue through Denny's folds. By the whimper she got in response, she knew it wouldn't take long before Denny exploded.

For a moment, Rachel considered taking her sweet time, extending the torture, but the truth of the matter was, she was as excited about Denny exploding as she was. All pretense gone, she lapped at Denny's need, sucking her clit into her mouth as she entered her with two fingers. Denny's hips rose off the bed as Rachel thrust inside of her, her tongue never letting up. It took all of Rachel's strength and maneuvering to not be bucked off the bed in Denny's growing excitement. She knew she was close so stilled her fingers deep inside, instead focusing all her attention on Denny's hard clit.

A high keening sound rent the air, Denny's body stilling and growing rigid. Rachel held on, her tongue flicking ruthlessly until her fingers were held prisoner by tightening muscles that clenched and unclenched. Suddenly a hand was on Rachel's head, pushing her mouth away. Rachel grinned, leaving a final kiss between Denny's legs before she gently eased her fingers out of their hot cocoon.

Kissing her way back up Denny's body, Rachel finally reached her lips, leaving a soft kiss there before snuggling in for a moment, allowing Denny to catch her breath. She hummed into the warmth of Denny's neck, her body pressed as closely to her side as she could. She was burning up inside, arousal to the point of painful.

"Jesus," Denny murmured finally, a hand coming up to cover her eyes.

Rachel grinned, lifting her head to look down at

her. "Enjoy that, did you?" she teased.

Denny glanced at her with a raised eyebrow. She grabbed one of Rachel's hands and put it into the copious wetness between her legs. "What do you think?"

"Maybe."

"Possibly?" Denny asked, lifting her head a bit to land a kiss.

"Potentially," Rachel murmured against those soft lips.

"Could be," Denny said before pushing Rachel to her back. Hovering over Rachel, she lowered her head until her lips grazed Rachel's ear. "How about a little FM 2 action?"

Rachel purred deep in her throat as she watched Denny get off the bed and open the drawer in the bedside table. Denny attached the leather harness before attaching their favorite dildo.

"Nothing like Food Masher's little sister," Rachel said with a grin, Denny chuckling as she climbed back on the bed, the dildo bobbing obscenely between her legs. She grabbed it and gently tugged until Denny was lying on top of her, the dildo pressed intimately against her. "Do you think Dean still has the original?" she murmured, bringing a smile to Denny's lips.

"Probably."

Any reply Rachel may have had was silenced as Denny began to slowly move her hips, the dildo sliding easily through her folds, rubbing against her clit with each pass. Rachel entangled her fingers into Denny's hair and brought her down for a slow kiss, their tongues caressing in rhythm with Denny's hips.

Rachel sighed into Denny's mouth, her legs falling open further as she allowed her body to fully feel the pleasure, her wetness and readiness growing. She reached down between them and took hold of the slick phallus and guided it to her opening, Denny doing the rest with the slow push of her hips. Rachel felt so full, so content as Denny lay her body flush with hers, their hips pressed tightly together.

The kiss continued as Denny began a slow thrust, the dildo easily sliding within Rachel's slick depths. Rachel traced lazy patterns down a strong back before cupping Denny's behind, which flexed in response. She loved the feel of their breasts pressed together, softness upon softness. Not for the first time, she wondered how on earth she had ever been not only married to, but intimate with Matt. Being with Denny in every way was so natural, so beautiful and so *right*.

She looked up into Denny's beautiful face as Denny pushed up on her hands, increasing the speed and strength of her thrusts a bit. Rachel moved her hips with her, groaning deep in her throat as the pleasure began to build. She could tell by Denny's flushed features that she was feeling it, too. Rachel lifted her spread knees a bit, allowing for deeper penetration as the thrusts got harder and faster.

It didn't take long before Denny's hips were slapping against Rachel's, the bed protesting with every hard thrust. Rachel's moans and whimpers were constant as her nails dug into Denny's flesh, her body readying itself for the explosion that was building between her legs. Finally, her release came with a deafening cry that echoed within the walls of the room, Denny following moments later, her head thrown back before she buried her face in Rachel's neck.

Rachel clung to Denny, who collapsed on top of her, their bodies pressed as close as possible. She hugged her close, chest heaving as her heart pounded in time with the pulsing between her legs. She brought a hand up and buried it into Denny's hair, holding her head against her. She could feel Denny's hot breath against her skin and then a soft kiss placed there before Denny raised her head. Their gazes met and something so profound passed between them that Rachel felt it to her very soul.

Smiling, she gave Denny a small nod. "I know," she whispered. "I love you, too."

They shared a small kiss before Rachel was hugged to Denny, held fast and steady in her arms. "I'll never do that again," Denny murmured. "Please don't sic Dean on me again."

Rachel laughed, giving Denny a quick kiss. "Then don't give me a reason to."

Kim Pritekel lives in Colorado and has been writing since she was 9 years old. She's an author and filmmaker. Her greatest passion in life is creating and the beautiful Rocky Mountains. She can be reached on Facebook or at www.kimpritekel.com.

Our Mother's Daughters

By Beth Burnett

My daughter, sitting across the table from me, is uncomfortable, and for some reason, that makes me want to be even more outrageous. She's so beautiful and she's just starting to come into her own. I don't have a lot of regrets in life and even now, I don't think I regret letting my parents raise her. She had a stable life with them and I got to be the fun mom who breezed in from my adventures to visit and hear about her life in Ohio. Still, being raised by my conservative, wealthy parents has had its effects. She can be so judgmental. I'm looking forward to laying this bomb on her.

"I had my first lesbian experience," I say, grinning.

"Oh my god," she yelled. "Is everyone on this planet getting laid except for me?"

She clasps her hands over her mouth, aware that she has attracted the attention of several people around us. Laughing at her discomfort, I try to soothe her.

"Oh sweetie, come on. It's not that big a deal."

I don't know why it took me sixty years to have sex with a woman. After all, sixty is an age most people consider old, especially for women. Our children see us as sexless crones and society views us as reaching the end of our usefulness. I never believed the lies about older women. Maybe it's because I lived on communes several times and saw the way older women were just as viable and vibrant as the rest of the community. Or maybe it's because I went to the Michigan Womyn's Music festival when I was a young girl and realized that women of all ages were strong.

Davey shifts, looking pained. "Leah, let's be quite clear here. I do not have a problem with you having sex with a woman. I don't have a problem with you having sex with anyone. I just don't really want the details."

Sometimes I can't imagine how this child came out of my womb. She's so uptight.

"Sheila says you act repressed as a sort of strange rebellion against my ultra-free spirit."

She raises her voice again. "Just because I don't want to sit around with a bunch of women looking at my snatch in the mirror does not make me repressed."

The waitress slides in to bring our food. Sheila is a great woman and has taught me a lot about raising my feminist consciousness. I know the idea of studying our own anatomy is laughable to this younger generation but they don't know what it was like to be a woman in the 60s and the 70s. We had to fight for all of these things they take for granted. Learning to love our bodies was an important way to take control of them.

Davey leans over her hummus, smiling. "So did you like it?"

That's the question. Did I enjoy it? I'd made out with women before. Women were always more interesting to me than men, even from a young age. I had never found men and their lack of empathy to be appealing. I didn't want to end up someone's wife like my mother. I believe in living life on my own terms. Even when I was a small child, I wanted to experience everything, much to my parent's dismay. I wanted to climb every tree, sled down every hill, and talk to every person. As I got older, I wanted to kiss and cuddle and love everyone. Still, I knew that I wasn't a lesbian. The thrill of conversation with women was there, but not the body thrills. As a self-proclaimed fierce feminist, it would have made sense for me to be a lesbian, but it just wasn't in the stars.

"I liked it when she was doing me. Then again, that always has been my favorite part of sex. I hate giving blow jobs and the penetration part is usually over so fast. It doesn't do much for me. Always insist that a man go down on you before you do him, Davey, because once he gets it in you, it's all about him."

She sighs, looking appalled. I've always tried to be radically honest with my daughter. When I got pregnant at sixteen, I was flummoxed. I knew about birth control, of course, though what I knew I had learned from my own jaunts into Planned Parenthood to ask for information. My mother's only sex talk with me consisted of telling me that someday I would marry a good man and learn about the joys of being a wife. We were just starting to hear about the dangerous side effects of the pill, but I swear I still took it every day. I knew I didn't want to have the stilted, superficial relationship with Davey that I had with my own mother so I made it a practice to talk to my daughter about everything.

"So," she finally says. "Are you and Sheila an item now?"

Laughing, I shake my head. Sheila is a sexy woman, that's a fact. Skinny to the point of bony with a sharp jaw and a full mouth. She's brilliant and weird and I adore her. But... "Oh hell no. I'm not a lesbian.

No, it was fun but we're going to have to just be good friends."

"Hey now you can make another check mark on your bucket list."

"Exactly. It just wasn't my cup of tea. Besides, I really wasn't very good at it. I have a good understanding of where the clitoris is but for some reason, once I had my face buried down there, I just couldn't really find it with my tongue."

I'm well aware that Davey is in shock. I'm also aware of the stares from the tables around us. I'm so tired of feeling that I'm too much, that who I am is an embarrassment. I love my daughter, but sometimes, her judgment makes me want to shock her even more. Sometimes, I want to knock her out of that shell and help her see that life is about living, not about what other people think. She's looking sidelong at the next table, so I decide to up my game.

"Anyway, I kind of just put my finger in her and then stuck my tongue out and flailed around for a while until she started to moan."

The man next to us is openly staring, but I focus on my salad, ignoring him.

Davey clears her throat several times. She's blushing from shoulders to forehead and for a moment, I almost feel sorry for her. She is my daughter, after all. I loved her from the first moment I saw her. And I wanted to teach her how to be a free spirit and a fierce feminist. I figured I would sling her on my back and take her hiking and I would read to her from the classic female writers. She would grow up brilliant and feisty and strong and she would eventually fall in love with an equally strong woman and I'd proudly introduce my lesbian daughter to everyone.

Sadly, she turned out to be straight and a little narrow. Still, her best friend is a lesbian and I like to think that my teachings had something to do with that.

She's muttering about my parents now, wanting me to go see them. I wave my hand at her, dismissing the idea. My parents had no time for me as a kid, and they certainly couldn't care less for me as an adult.

"Leah, they do love you, you know. And they're not getting any younger."

"They'll be fine," I answer. "They'll probably outlive me."

The idea of my parents dying stops me for a second. They're old, after all. Old and sometimes frail. The last time I was there, my mother had a new shade of platinum hair color and she looked trim and fit in her tennis whites, but there was no denying that she looked like an old lady. A healthy old lady, but an old lady nonetheless.

Davey is still looking at me, wanting me to agree to visit them. I shake my head. "We better get going. Sheila and I want to have a get together with a few of the ladies from class. Now that I know you're not going to be home, I can have it at our place."

She leaves money on the bill tray and I gather my purse. Sensing the eyes of the people from the next table, I decide to leave them all with something to gossip about with their straight-laced friends later.

"Incidentally," I add, standing proudly. "The great thing about a strap-on is that it stays hard and erect forever." I whip around, catching the eyes of the man at the next table. "And no jizz."

Tugging my purse strap over my shoulder, I whirl on my heel and march toward the door, leaving them all staring after me.

Beth Burnett is a full time grad student, writer, teacher, and women's empowerment coach. After living all over the country and the Caribbean, she finally settled down in Michigan where she writes, plays with her pets, hikes, reads, and tries to grow vegetables with the dubious help of a ground hog named Sal. Beth is currently working on her fourth novel, Eating Life.
http://wwww.bethsnewlife.com

Soul Mates in Prose

By Elizabeth M. Hodge

I saw the years of my life spaced along a road in the form of telephone poles threaded together by wires...I couldn't see a single pole beyond the nineteenth. Sylvia Plath, **The Bell Jar**

Preface

Some things are, indeed, emblematic of ones life. A battered, much abused copy of Sylvia Plath's **The Bell Jar** follows me through each transformation, each incarnation of who I think that I am. Secrets whisper, through the musty, dog-eared pages. Those secrets, still wrap around my psyche–ever present, persistent, replicating cyclically. Liz, still masquerading, with much lauded potential that she cannot believe, perches, tenses, and quivers–fearing any forward motion, choking on what could be, what is, what was, instead of actually living. Within those pages, rests an implicit truth, one that underlies each day, regardless of how many facades I've learned to wear. That paperback found its way into my room when I was nineteen and extremely suicidal, twins with the main character, Esther. Obviously, I have avoided successful suicide, since I am writing this at 50; however, I continue to feel the threading of my life and the unresolved sadness that persists.

Past to Present

After being unceremoniously banished from the Navy – or more aptly: flogged, tarred, and branded with the letter "Q," I crept back to Ohio with all my meager possessions in tow. Woefully unprepared to cope with the nightmares of the what had just occurred, let alone contend with being sent back home; back to the place that I tried to escape. The place where old wounds still oozed. Home, where the conflict of being a white trash girl yet brillant. The weirdo surging with potential, who victoriously managed accolades in a prep school for academically gifted, while knowing, that free lunch, welfare girls didn't belong anywhere, Inhaling sneers of classmates, holding in the secrets of daily shame, all the while soaking in any knowledge that might help me escape the life of an indentured servant to poverty, violence, alcoholism, and loneliness. Back to the place where the misfit me believed that scholastic aptitude would propel me to any university until the senior year, when the folly was exposed. So I fled. Lunging into an "A-J Squared Away" future plan on my eighteenth birthday – signing my soul to the military on water – just to get away, to have a job that was not McDonald's, and to have a shot at college despite being a philosophically inclined, social justice minded kid with socialist tendencies (as well as an untested, but probable lesbian).

Contrariness just filled the bill – at least for that day, and I signed the papers. Five days passed after graduation, and while my classmates went off to Europe, the Coast, or the pool, I climbed on board a plane for the first time and landed in the third rung of Hell, Orlando, in the summer, for boot camp. Eight weeks passed at the grinder of individuality, boot camp. Always striving to be the best, even in sweat and the folding of things, I was meritoriously promoted, second in my class. Fantastic! Except, then I discovered that the promise of recruiters for professional school was fiction. No language school-cum-spy school for me, regardless of the ASVAB scores, grades, and good manners.

I was placed three buildings down, still in Orlando, for advanced training (read: extended boot camp with carpentry and fire fighting skills added. Helpful that – a potential career as a firefighter for the girl with nightmares of burning at the stake!) Time passed, I was again meritoriously promoted, again second in my class (why always second?) when hit with lies number two and three – women are never sent to ships and placement "choices" are irrelevant. (Sure, give a kid from Ohio hopes of going somewhere cool with a preferential placement form: Europe, Asia, San Francisco, all places I dreamt of going. Of course I selected any place else but here.) So off I went to the **USS LY Spear**, based in Norfolk, VA – not SF or the UK, and but one hour by plane from Ohio. This proved to be an even lower rung of Hell for which the word "unprepared" merely skims the edges of the situation's depravity. Still, I managed to take another test, get promoted again, and become the Captain's flunky, all the while threading along the needle of evil's tapestry. Without exploring the multitude of soul crushing details, I was cast out, given a bus ticket, Ohio bound, minus one stripe, a few pieces of flesh, and the last few remnants of my innocence – dignity long since stolen

40

away. Oh, and now not only did I have to explain to my family why I'm coming home so soon - it's been not quite a year, after all - but I have to come out, find a job, kick my sister out of my bedroom, find civilian clothes, and face that horrible apartment in the housing projects – roaches, noise, violence and all. Yay me! Oh, did I mention that my sister sold all of my clothes and everything else that I had left behind? Heavy sigh.

Sliding past a few months of miserable detail, I landed a job at a pharmacy in the nice neighborhood where my grandparents, other relatives, and former classmates lived: all who had lives that I deeply envied. Around the corner from the Pharmacy was a bookstore – Drew's – where I wandered each day during my lunch break. Each Friday I spent a portion of my paycheck, collecting all the books that would extend my intellectual life beyond the college literature classes I yearned to take. Truth be told, I got the idea from the movie, "The Days of Wine and Roses" where the main character read the entire encyclopedia set as a substitute for her college education. At any rate, I devoured every work by classic Russian, French, German, British, and of course, American authors, while at the same time, allowing myself to indulge on a few that were not precisely classic, but spoke to me in a special, usually dark and twisted way. Sylvia Plath, my kindred spirit in high school, became my soul mate in my new, attic (okay, I called it a garret) room. The Bell Jar, pushing the heterosexual elements aside, told so much of my story - it was my story. Even the cover page held my gaze.

The main character, an insecure over achiever, cannot tell of her secret shame, her mental fragility, to any one, for fear of being institutionalized, not just misunderstood. Her mother, like mine, was domineering, her loneliness, so palpable, resonated with mine. Each line, I underscored or starred, I bent pages, dog-earring the ideas for further examination. Afterward I wrote pages and pages in my journal – exploring the ideas exploring my own desperate, angry, lonely head-space. Still craving an outlet for the ideas exploding within, poetry began pouring out of my fingertips – symbolic, esoteric, often morose, an extension of journaling, an effort to loose the crowded thoughts from my angry, unfulfilled mind. Plath, her words, poetry and journals, helped prop me up, next to my other companion, Virginia Woolf (whose journals, letters, and novels sustained me) and kept me from following their destructive path. I could feel their despair and journey into their darkness, so I didn't need to actually experience it myself. Re-reading, touching – not cradling the book, smelling my own fear and angst in the yellowing pages, I could tether my being to that rickety desk which held my secrets, and not succumb to the urge to ultimately escape. While suicide held a kind of reasonableness to it, the potential that rested – no bristled - within me, did not want to follow that logic – yet. The yearning for recognition, redemption from self-loathing, fear of both success and failure resound within her works and within myself. All I have to do is open the book and I am transported to that garret room, to the lamp lit desk, to that lost young woman in 1982 and to that lost middle aged woman of today. Few writers have such an impact on me, for few writers, oddly, feel not like kindred spirits so much as a mirror, of sorts. Sylvia Plath died a month prior to my own birth and I used to believe, ever so slightly, that I held her re-incarnated spirit. Perhaps that's a stretch of sorts, but it's a belief that I continue to ponder.

The End

Elizabeth M Hodge fashions complex stories in a minimalist style. Her first poetry collection, <u>Undone</u>, garnered a Goldie in 2015. In addition to poetry, she enjoys writing short fiction. Elizabeth holds advanced degrees in Philosophy, Women's Studies, and Education. She left academia to pursue writing.

Mercy Lost

By Shelia Powell and Liz McMullen

"A child is a promise, and hiding the truth from Alessandro will bring great sadness." Mirela pressed the damp cloth on the mother's forehead; four hours of labor were about to come to an end, but the price for this birth will be paid for decades. She knew Lucia didn't mean to defy the King. What she did not know was how this child would affect her magic, and the magic of her husband.

"It's a baby, our baby, how could I regret her birth?" Plump tears slipped down her face. "We won't lose all of our powers, will we?"

Mirela didn't have to heart to tell her the truth—they would not only lose their powers the day Alessandro discovered their deception, they would lose their souls and damn Mercy to a life a servitude. These are not things to tell a woman gripped with pain. She would find out soon enough.

Lucia screamed through her next contraction. Mirela examined the young woman; the baby would be here soon. Part of Mirela admired her strength, and her desire to give birth to Mercy in a way that most women didn't these days. There were no monitors blipping or doctors being paged over the loud speaker. The room was cozy and warm…and calm after she had kicked Stephano out. The frantic adult version of "are we there yet" was only putting more stress on the mother. She would let him back in to cut the cord.

When the baby finally crowned, Lucia cried with relief. Mercy was on her way, and more quickly than Mirela expected. She caught the babe just in time. Instead of crying, Mercy looked Mirela right in the eye and cooed. Mirela's eyes widened as the child waved her arm and the door opened. Stephano collapsed into the room.

"What, what is it? Is there something wrong?" Lucia was frantic, and Stephano barely restrained his desire to snatch his daughter up.

"There is nothing wrong with little Mercy. She's more powerful than I anticipated."

Stephano did his part, then swaddled his daughter. Lucia cried as she held her first born, in happiness and relief.

Mirela would explain the rest later. They deserved this moment. She left their joy undisturbed.

❧❧❧❧

Seven years later, Mirela helped Nicolo into this world. This time, there would be no bliss, no joy, only terror. Mirela had warned them, but they shushed her off, thinking that she worried too much. The door to their bedroom opened, and the future she had seen came to life in full living color.

"Bring the child to me," Alessandro demanded.

Stephano froze, then cuddled little Nicolo close.

Kaiden and Klare entered the room. Their dark hair and deeply tanned skin suited the King's enforcers. They were as dark as the death they brought into this world.

"Or would you prefer Kaiden snatch the squalling babe from your arms?"

Lucia was shaking, from the absence of the baby inside of her and the fear that Alessandro would take him away forever. "Please, he's just a little boy."

In three large steps, Alessandro was at Stephano's side. "Give me the babe, now." He did not shout; his whispers were far more terrifying.

A swirl of witch wind grew into a tempest. Young Mercy had arrived. "Get away from my family!" Her little voice didn't match the chaos her magic was creating.

Alessandro raised his hand, then tensed his fist. The wind died down immediately.

Mercy's large brown eyes widened in shock. "How did you—"

"I didn't know you had witch wind, little girl, but I do know something more important. You see things when you touch them, am I right?"

"Yes," Mercy replied. Her lower lip started to quiver, but she did not cry. At least, not yet.

Mirela had backed away. She would not run from the room, but she could not be close to what was about to happen.

"My daughters Kaiden and Klare have killed thousands. If they touch you, you will see each and every one of their victims die. Even if they let go, you will see the dead they've dealt in your dreams."

Mercy did cry; she was trembling. "I'll be good," she promised.

At the end of his patience, he called the baby into his arms, then rested his hand on the newborn's forehead. "I feel nothing," Alessandro said in shock. A darkness crossed his face, far more terrifying than his rage.

"My baby is dead?" Lucia nearly got up from bed to check, but Alessandro held her in place with just one finger.

"Not yet. Have you strayed from your husband?"

"No!" both parents shouted at once.

Alessandro closed his eyes and focused on the child. "This child belongs to you both, yes, but how is it that he is powerless?"

"Powerless?" Lucia was desperate to check on her baby, to take him back, but she knew better. The tears that slipped down her face were of impotent rage.

"This is an ordinary boy." Alessandro tossed the baby and Stephano nearly tripped over his own feet when he lunged to catch him.

"Mirela, you've been keeping secrets." Alessandro turned his cold blue eyes on her.

Mirela stood still and said nothing. She knew what would come next, but she could do nothing else. Her death would follow theirs. She would not flinch and would not cry. She knew they would all have to pay this price. Mirela looked at Mercy, wishing she could cover the girl's eyes.

Alessandro waved his hand and smoke engulfed the room. When it cleared, they were someplace far more terrifying than a house fire. They were in Alessandro's throne room. "Cuff the girl first."

When Klare started toward the girl, Mirela called for her to stop. "I will do it, your majesty." She walked over to the girl and held her close. "Now, Mercy, these are enchanted shackles. They will make it impossible to use magic against them."

"No."

"Yes, sweet girl." She pulled her close and locked the cuffs. "Close your eyes, baby girl. That's the best that you can do."

Mercy tried to squirm away, but she couldn't. Her mother tried to soothe her from a distance. "Listen to Mirela, honey. This will be over soon."

Mirela took the baby from Stephano. "I will hold him, he will be safe, and he will not remember."

Stephano's brown eyes were red rimmed as he nodded his head. "Okay."

He kissed his baby goodbye, and Lucia cuddled him close for long moments then finally gave him up. "I'm so sorry, *piccolo angelo*."

Mirela let herself cry as she walked away from the young couple. She hated what she was forced to do, but both parents knew their deception would end this way.

"Kaiden, Klare, restrain the prisoners," Alessandro demanded. The dagger he pulled from its scabbard was long, thin, and deceptively dull. "Lucia, you know what this knife can do. Why don't you explain it to your dear *powerful* daughter?"

Lucia shook her head. "No, I will not terrorize my child."

"Of course not. Why would I deny my sweet daughters a most worthy target?"

"No, don't let those monsters touch Mercy," Lucia cried.

Stephano struggled against Klare's grip. "She's just a girl. Close your eyes, honey, please do as I ask."

"But Daddy..." The six-year-old lost her battle with her tears. She was sobbing and nearly breathless.

"I love you, baby. Mommy and Daddy will always love you. Please close your eyes now." Stephano tried to keep the tears from his voice, but failed. His heart was breaking.

"You seem to think you are in charge. Mercy will not be able to close her eyes, not even if she tried." Alessandro stepped closer to Lucia and Stephano. "You knew keeping this secret would come at a price. This little girl sucked up most of your powers, so much so that poor Nicolo has none."

"What does he mean, Mama?"

Lucia didn't have the heart to answer with anything more than a whispered, "I'm sorry."

"This knife steals powers." Alessandro walked to Mercy's side and showed her the deadly implement. "They had no right to give most of theirs to you. Their magic belongs to me." He spoke with the darkness that belongs to true evil.

"Magic is a gift from the Gods. You can't take it away," Mercy insisted.

"And who told you I was not a God?"

"Nnnn…no one."

Alessandro stabbed Stephano first; the knife glowed as it sucked the lingering magic from his body. Klare dropped him to the stone floor.

"Daddy, noooooo."

Another swift jab stole Lucia's magic.

"Mmaamamamaamamdadadaddaddy."

Mirela's heart was breaking; seeing their deaths in a vision was nothing compared to watching it happen in real life. The hardest part was knowing that Alessandro was not quite done yet.

"Kaiden, finish it."

Kaiden held Lucia up. She was not quite dead yet; neither was Stephano, who was now held to Klare's chest. The enforcers dragged their victims to stand right in front of the child.

Mirela almost closed her eyes, but she did not deserve that mercy. She must see it all.

With a flick of their wrists, cursed blades appeared in the hands of the executioners. The blades were mean, yet hauntingly beautiful. Kaiden held the sapphire encrusted handle with the delicate precision of a surgeon. Klare was prone to theatrics, so her blade was incrusted with blood diamonds, from the handle up through the long curved steel.

Blood sprayed in two arcs as Kaiden and Klare removed their heads. It splattered the child. Mirela tensed; she couldn't imagine the horror of losing both parents and then seeing their lives through with brutal clarity, thanks to her psychometry magic. Even seeing happy memories could hurt.

Mercy was in shock. She was pale, barely breathing.

Two beautiful orbs of light left their bodies and were captured in a box. Alessandro closed the ornate box with a cruel snap. "These are the souls of your mother and father. If you ever think to use your magic against me or anyone in my kingdom, I will send your parents to hell."

Mercy was shaking violently as she crumpled to the floor. She was crying hysterically, and Mirela ached to go to her.

"Looks like you have gone from midwife to governess. This squalling brat is yours to care for, in the tower of course. You'll find it quite cozy. Guards, take her to the turret. She'll like it there. A full view of the kingdom as far as your old wizened eyes can see."

"But, I thought…"

"No, I won't kill you, not when I need this tiny little ordinary child to keep the powerful one in line.

Now off with you, out of my sight."

Mercy watched Mirela go. The old woman carried the last part of Mercy's family with her. She wanted her magic. She wanted to bring her mama and papa back, but these bracelets wouldn't let her.

"You, my special one, will be kept much closer." Alessandro gestured to Klare, who was wiping her bloody blade on Stephano's shirt. "Take her to the guest room beside my chamber."

Klare nodded.

"She won't touch you, even if you disobey."

Mercy blinked her eyes. She couldn't think through her terror.

"I have your worthless brother and the souls of your parents. If you misbehave, try to run away, or hurt *anyone* without my permission, they will pay the price and you will still be my prisoner."

❧❧❧❧

When the thick lock clunked, Mercy was finally alone. She walked to the window and looked down at the garden. *How can the day be so pretty?* She sobbed so hard her teardrops plinked and pooled on the stone windowsill. The puddle started to glow. Mercy jumped back in horror. "What is that?"

When the glow turned into a ball of flame, she shrieked in terror. The ball of fire shifted, shimmering into a looking glass. Through the glass, she saw a cheerful kitchen with people that she had never seen before. A tall older woman, whose white hair made her look like an angel, pulled a sheet of chocolate chip cookies from the oven. A little girl with wild red curls clapped her hands in excitement. Mercy gasped when the she touched the hot pan.

To Mercy's shock, the little girl didn't burn herself.

"Nana 'Fia, I'z a fiwer starter, I not get burndeded," the little girl said.

"Of course not, Firefly, but the cookies need to cool. Otherwise they break up and make a mess."

Another woman scooped up the little girl and held her. She had hair so long, she was almost Rapunzel. Her pretty red hair was curly. Mercy reached out to touch a lock. When she did, the image shimmered and disappeared.

A hand covered her mouth, and to her surprise, she saw nothing. No past, no evil thoughts, *nothing*. The shock stilled her struggling. When she relaxed, the person released her.

The woman before her looked so strange. Her eyes were nearly translucent with veins of violet. She was pale. Her long blond hair was even whiter than the woman in her vision. She was a killer, that much Mercy knew, but she was unafraid.

The woman nodded, then introduced herself. "I'm Scarlett." She paused, then took a seat at the table. Now she didn't seem so tall and cold.

Mercy blinked once, then twice. The skin of her lids were raw from tears. "How did you get past the guard?" Mercy was curious about something else. Ever since she could remember, when someone touched her, she could see their thoughts, their memories, their hopes…and sometimes, really bad stuff. "How come I didn't feel anything when you covered my mouth?"

"I knew of your gift, and your loss. I didn't want to scare you with my memories. I wanted you to feel safe, so I blocked your magic." Scarlett huffed out a breath, disturbing the few strands that had worked free from her tight braid. "I am going to tell you something scary, but I promise I will never hurt you."

The little girl nodded. She had seen so much that day. What could this woman possibly tell her that could be more horrible than watching her mommy and daddy die and her baby brother kidnapped?

Scarlett pursed her lips, then continued, "I am a spy. I steal secrets."

"That's not so scary," Mercy insisted.

"Sometimes I kill people."

Mercy flinched and recoiled.

"Please don't…" Scarlett reached for her, but let her hand drop limply at her side. "I kill bad people, and I save good people, when I can."

"Are you here to kill the King?"

"That's not something I am able to do right now." Scarlett held up her hand to stop Mercy from asking more questions. "I've come to rescue you."

"I can't leave. The King said he would do horrible things. I can't make him mad." Mercy banged her balled fists against her sides. "You need to go."

Scarlett smiled.

Mercy gave her a cross look. "Why are you smiling at me?"

"You're strong. I like to see that in a girl." Scarlett reached into the leather pouch secured to her belt. She had the box. "These belong to you."

Mercy reached for the box and to her surprise, Scarlett gave it to her. The handcuffs may have stopped her from using magic, but she knew this was the right box. She opened it and the shining orbs caught her eye. She could smell her mama's jasmine perfume and her father's pipe smoke. She gently closed the lid. She was full of questions and anger. "How did you get this so fast? Why, why didn't you save Mama and Papa before they killed them?"

Scarlett closed her eyes, then spoke, "I am sorry we were too late. We were about to jump in when Alessandro threw the smokescreen." The sadness in Scarlett's eyes shifted into a serious expression. "My friends Kayla and Lilith are getting Mirela and Nicolo. We will escape once I know they are safe."

"Too late. Too late." Mercy felt so helpless and sad. She crumpled to the floor and began to tremble and cry.

"Oh, please don't cry. May I comfort you?"

Mercy was not sure what she meant, but she nodded.

Scarlett joined her on the floor, then opened her arms. Mercy crawled into her lap. She didn't feel so strong anymore. Mercy wanted to sleep. This was the time of day Mama put her down for a nap. Maybe if she took a nap, she could wake up and everything would be all better. Scarlett made shushing sounds, and rocked her until the crying stopped.

"I want my mommy, I want my daddy. Can you bring them back?" She tried to give the fancy box back to Scarlett. "Here, take these and put them back inside them. Then we can all go home."

"I can't bring them back, little one." Tears, like liquid crystal, ran down Scarlett's cheek.

Mercy wiped away tears and hugged Scarlett.

"Thank you, little one. That was kind." Scarlett smoothed down Mercy's hair.

Scarlett started rock her again, and she was growing very sleepy. She burrowed in closer as the woman sang to her; she smelled fresh, like spring rain. Mercy could barely keep her eyes open. Even if she couldn't read Scarlett's mind, she knew she was true. She felt safe, very warm and safe.

"Sleep, little one. When you wake, you will be far from this castle. The little girl in your vision will share one of those chocolate chip cookies when you get there." Mercy heard those last words before she fell into a deep, dreamless sleep.

Liz McMullen is an author, mentor, publisher, and documentarian. Her debut novel, If I Die Before I Wake, *was a Rainbow Award Finalist. She has co-authored* the Finding Home Series *with good friend Sheila Powell.*

Shelia Powell is a well-known psychic medium empath. She has bee featured on the Travel Channel's "Ghost Adventures" *and* "Ghost Adventures Aftershocks." *She is working on the* Finding Home *series with her friend and co-author Liz McMullen.*

Just Jump

By Leslie Murray

Jenny MacKenzie watched as the open grassy field that they would land on rapidly approached. She no longer feared jumping out of a plane. The warmth and security of Seven's body strapped tightly to her back was like a balm for her soul, even though her adrenaline was still making her muscles twitch and her breathing come quickly. Her lover had proposed to her, slipped a ring on her finger, then shoved them both out of the plane, effectively shifting her focus from fear to elation with one small push.

She screamed her acceptance of the proposal, then laughed and woohoo'd herself hoarse during the free fall, but once the bright blue canopy of their parachute opened, she calmed considerably and relaxed enough to enjoy the ride. The ground coming up was not nearly as interesting to look at as the gleaming platinum band placed around her finger not five minutes before. She could hardly believe that a small piece of jewelry that never seemed to mean much to her before was instantly the most important thing in her life.

Jenny tucked an errant bit of blonde hair back under her helmet and adjusted her goggles over gleeful green eyes. She thought briefly of trying to close her mouth, afraid of catching bugs in her teeth, but her huge smile won out. She was twenty-five years old, and an unemployed doctor with a considerable amount of student loans, but none of that mattered. She had never been happier.

Finding Seven again after they were separated as kids was the best thing that ever happened to her. Little by little, as the years passed, Jenny grew less dependent on the memory of their childhood friendship, but having Seven in her life again had thrown open windows she hadn't realized she'd closed. At a time in her life when she was searching for something missing within, her friend had reappeared. Gravely injured and dying, she had saved Seven's life deep in the Bolivian wilderness and in the process had found the other half of her soul.

Jenny turned her head to look at Seven as best she could. The elation she felt was reflected back at her in the sparking blue of her companion's eyes. The thrill of the jump and the prospect of spending their lives together was overwhelming and wonderful for them both.

"The touch down is the trickiest part. Here we go!" Seven shouted as she turned the parachute into the wind. "I'm going to pull on the toggles, which will slow down our forward motion enough to land."

Jenny nodded her understanding.

"Tuck up your knees! Let me take the landing!" Jenny did as instructed and soon they were sliding along the ground on Seven's butt. She twisted in the confines of the harness to see Seven grinning from ear to ear.

Jenny began tugging at the straps with frantic energy. "Get me out of this thing, Sev! I need to give you a proper kiss, right now!"

Seven laughed as the parachute drifted over their heads and floated to rest a few feet in front of them. She stood them up and wrapped Jenny in a hug from behind before two sets of hands worked to release the various straps and buckles. Once free, Jenny turned and launched herself into Seven's arms, planting wet kisses all over her face and goggles. Seven sat back down with a thump and a lap load of excited fiancé. "I can't believe you just did that," Jenny said between kisses, laughing.

"I thought it would be harder for you to say no if your life was in my hands at the moment of asking," Seven said, barely able to get the words out between Jenny's arduous assault.

"Wascally Wabbit." The kisses continued. "You're such a closet romantic. Why don't you pull that parachute over us and I'll show you how much I love you, right here in this field."

"As enticing as that sounds, I'm not sure how much fun it would be to get tangled in the lines while rolling around in a pile of red ants," Seven teased.

"What?" Jenny flew to her feet, frantically swatting at her pant legs. "We landed in an ant hill? God, I hate those things." She was about to go after Seven's pants too when she realized the woman had been joking.

Seven grinned at her lover's antics and stood up, preparing to gather the parachute. She would repack it later when they got back to the hangar. Jenny stood with her hands on her hips, glaring at her, but she couldn't hide the smile in her eyes.

A small truck was on the way across the field to pick them up as she bundled the lines. "So what did you think of the jump? Would you like to get certified and go solo with me sometime?"

Jenny wrapped her arms around Seven's waist and hugged her tight. She noticed again how perfectly they seemed to fit together as she tucked her head under the taller woman's chin. "I'll jump with you again, but only if we do it like that. Something about having you attached to me made it wonderful. I'm not sure I would like it as much otherwise."

Seven removed her helmet and goggles and ran her fingers through long hair the color of strong coffee. "I liked it too." Her cool blue eyes sparkled as she bent her tall frame and captured Jenny's lips in a playful kiss.

A door slammed on the pickup truck and the driver cleared his throat. "Sorry to rush you along, ladies, but I got another pair of jumpers waiting for me back at the hangar," the driver said, not unkindly.

Jenny unclipped and removed her helmet, taking one last look at their surroundings. It was a cloudless and unseasonably warm fall day and she wanted to remember every detail. She took Seven's hand in hers as they made their way toward the waiting vehicle. "Know what I'm looking forward to most right now?"

"White dress? Big party? Sex in front of the fireplace?" Seven smirked.

"Well, yes to all of those, but that's not what I was referring to specifically." Jenny swatted her playfully in the stomach. "Now I'm going on a mission to find you the perfect ring, and I can't wait."

"Want some company?"

"Nope. I want it to be a surprise. Like you did for me."

"Ho boy. All righty, but nothing too traditional,

okay? Gigantic diamonds might give away my position if I'm on a mission." She smiled. Jenny knew enough about this woman by now to know what she did and didn't like. Seven didn't do bling.

❧ ❧ ❧ ❧

Some time later in the blackest dark of night, Seven Michelis awoke on the couch of their Alexandria, Virginia townhouse. She wasn't sure what woke her but assumed it was either her tingling arm, asleep due to the blonde head resting on it, or the disturbing dream she couldn't quite remember. Her eyes took in the shadows and dark corners of the room as she willed her rapidly beating heart to slow. She felt wide awake, alert, and ready for danger though she knew none was forthcoming.

Seven sighed deeply and settled her body back into the soft cushions of the couch. The embers in the fireplace glowed dimly, the flames burned out long ago, but just looking at the mercurial shifting of warm colors helped to calm her suddenly frayed nerves. It was the dream that had upset her rest.

She felt discontent. She was naked, sated, and had the love of her life wrapped in her arms sleeping peacefully, but still, her head would not rest. For the last several days, her emotions had been all over the place. She was hesitant to leave the house because she didn't want to be around other people, unable to put any serious thought to her future with the government, and had trouble sleeping. She felt scattered and confused. It seemed her only solace was found in Jenny's warm embrace.

Seven had always known what her future held.

As a former Marine Scout Sniper now working for a covert government agency, she was a planner who appreciated the confidence that came with knowing what was next. She may have rushed proposing to Jenny a bit, considering they had only been together a short while, but having this amazing woman in her life had given her strength and stability that grounded her and made her happier than she ever thought possible.

She was beginning to come to terms with the fact that her traumatic failure and the loss of Marcus had left her in worse shape than she originally thought. Her experience in Bolivia had damaged her, and Jenny was the cure. The bullet wounds from her failed mission had long since healed, but Seven could still feel the tightness of the scars. The pulling sensation often caught her off guard and sent her thoughts back to the desperation and anguish she felt as she ran for her life. Cold, wet, and bleeding out, the vision of Marcus being shot in the head, failure, guilt, the thoughts assaulted her without warning. But when she opened her eyes, there was Jenny.

She stroked the young woman's hair gently so as not to wake her, breathed in her scent, and smiled fondly at the memory of their earlier activities. Jenny had kept her promise to show Seven exactly how much she loved her, and by god, it was a lot. She pressed a kiss to her forehead then readjusted slightly to relieve her sleeping arm. Jenny grunted at the disruption of her human pillow moving and snuggled in tighter.

"I can hear you thinking," she whispered sleepily.

"I was thinking if I were a shark, you would be my lamprey," Seven whispered back.

The bundle in her arms giggled then smacked her lips together a couple times and settled back in for sleep. "My feet are cold," she complained, never opening her eyes. Seven bent her long frame and tucked her own toes between the couch and cushions then adjusted the blanket over Jenny's feet.

"Better?"

"Mmm. Love you."

"Love you, too."

Seven looked around the dimly lit room and smiled at the changes that had taken place since Jenny moved in with her. There were new paintings over the mantle and bits of sculptured artwork here and there. Jenny loved art and her personal touches had filled in the gaps that made this place their home. She loved this woman with all her heart and would do anything to protect her. This thought caused something to stir in Seven, a wave of self-doubt that was against her very nature. She pinched her eyes shut and pulled her lover closer, pressing a kiss into her hair. She couldn't protect Marcus. How could she trust herself to protect Jenny?

As if sensing her disquiet, Jenny kissed her collarbone, her jaw, and then gave her a squeeze. It was as though she could read Seven's mind when she asked, seemingly out of nowhere, "Baby, did you ever think of me before?"

"Hmm?" Seven asked, bewildered by the question. An incident Seven remembered from her days as a Marine flashed through her mind. The innocent face of a little Iraqi girl she hadn't thought of in years suddenly flooded her memory, causing her anxiety to intensify. She shook her head as if to loosen its grip on her psyche.

Jenny rolled over and backed into the warm body behind her. "I was just wondering if you ever thought of me after you moved away. It was sixteen years before we found each other again. We wrote for a while, but I think we lost touch completely when I was about ten."

"Did you think of me?"

"Yeah. Less as I got older, but I never forgot you. At least a few times a year I would wonder where you were, what you were up to. I missed what we had. I never had a friend since you that I was as close to. Even in high school, I spent most of my time with my nose in a book. I had friends, but their girlish pursuits always seemed kind of juvenile to me. Sometimes, when I had a decision to make, I would ask myself, 'What would Seven do?'"

Seven chuckled. "And what would I say?"

"You always helped me keep my feet on the ground and make the responsible choices." Jenny rolled back over and stretched up for a kiss.

"And would responsible Seven suggest we move upstairs to bed so you could get a good night's rest?"

"No, she wouldn't."

"No?"

"No. She would kiss me a little bit more, then tell me the truth about whether or not she ever thought about me all those years apart."

Seven realized she was caught trying to dodge the original question. She sighed. There was no point in ever trying to distract Jenny once she had her mind set to something. She scootched down on the couch so they were face-to-face and complied with her request for a kiss. "The answer is yes," she said softly as she pushed an errant wisp of hair off Jenny's forehead. "I did think of you. In fact, there was one time in particular when I thought of little else for weeks. I even sat down to write you a letter, though I had no idea where to send it. I never finished the letter. Job got in the way."

"Did something happen to make you think of me?" Jenny asked impishly. She seemed almost bashful and sounded like a kid looking for confirmation of their friendship. "Did you dig through a shoebox of old stuff or something?"

Seven hesitated. Any thought or story that involved Marcus caused a pain in her heart. She wasn't sure she wanted to rehash yet another failure. When she looked back on her time as a Marine, she had no regrets about the enemies she'd dispatched. Her only regrets were for the innocent people she couldn't save.

"There was a little girl in Iraq. She reminded me of you."

"Did she have red hair and green eyes?"

Seven grinned at her lover, knowing full well she was being teased. "It wasn't her looks. She had dark hair and eyes like most of the other kids over there. Her personality captured my attention. She was a bossy little thing."

Jenny pinched Seven's butt and followed up with a playful smack to the same spot. "Who are you calling bossy?" She asked, with a mock glare.

Seven smiled adoringly and gave her a peck on the nose. "I would see her writing stories all the time. She would write in the sand, in the air; it was obvious she had a vivid imagination. She was always making up games to play with the other little boy who was with her. I think she would have been something special under different circumstances."

"Would have been?"

The sadness in Seven's expressive eyes answered Jenny's question.

"What was her name?" Jenny sat up and backed

into the corner of the couch. She encouraged Seven into her arms then wrapped them both in the blanket to ward off the night's chill.

They sat in silence for a moment as Seven let her thoughts fully return to those days in her life. "I don't know. I never met her," she said quietly.

Seven's eyes drifted back to the calm of the shifting embers. "Marcus and I had been deployed to Kuwait. It was well after the Persian Gulf War, but Saddam wasn't playing by the rules he'd agreed to, and the powers that be were getting pissed off. They wanted to send him a message in the form of some well-placed cruise missiles to try and get him back in line. He was producing weapons again, and the plan was to take out his plants. There was more going on, though. Instead of moving into Iraq and ridding the world of him once and for all, he was left to continue the systematic torture and murder of his own people. It was open season on any group he considered worthy of extermination."

Seven didn't often speak of her time as a Marine, preferring to keep the things she'd seen tucked away. It would be too easy for them to overwhelm her if she let it happen, but Jenny's soothing presence, the trust between them, and her soft touch eased her mind. "We had undercover people keeping an eye on his weapon production and troop activities, and it was ugly. There was this one hatchet man who was a real slippery psychopath. His game was to move into a village, kill all the men and women, then leave all the children alive to use as human shields. He'd kill them too, eventually, just before he moved on. He knew we wouldn't overtly come after him if there was a possibility of mass child casualties. Two times, we sent in SEAL teams to take him out. They thought the missions were successful, but then the bastard would show up somewhere else. He kept slipping away."

"I'm afraid to ask, but what does all that have to do with the girl that reminded you of me? Where do you fit in?"

"The commanders decided they would use the air strike as an opportunity to wipe this murderer out once and for all. What he was doing was sanctioned genocide, and I think we felt partially responsible since those people were basically left to defend themselves after the Gulf War ended.

"We received intel that Fedora - that's what we called him - was moving into an area near where we were stationed, so a small team of us were sent in to watch and wait. Our mission was to confirm the target's location and report back. They hoped to send in an air strike, timed with the plant bombings, before he had a chance to surround himself with the orphans he created."

"Tell me what happened."

The temperature was stifling even in the shade of their hide, the concealed position they'd chosen from where they would watch for their target. The dry, hard packed soil and prickly brush in the area they had dug in did little to alleviate the onslaught of the midday sun.

Seven's spotter and longtime partner, Marcus, busied himself configuring the bushes around them as she adjusted her rifle scope to focus on the small village compound a quarter mile ahead. They had crept close in the dark of night and found an ideal spot for surveillance. The rocky hill they were hiding on provided good cover and an excellent vantage point from which to observe the nearby activities.

Marcus dug through his pack and fished out two MREs. "Time to eat, Sev. We only have about a half hour before the patrol comes back around."

Seven settled her back against the boulder she was peering over and resigned herself to yet another foray into questionable foodstuffs. Marcus grinned wickedly as he chose which MRE he would keep and which he would give to Seven. "Meal Number Fifteen, Beef Enchiladas and Mexican Flavored Rice. Yummy. That one's definitely for you," he said with a quiet laugh.

Seven grimaced and pulled the pouch open, spreading the contents in her lap. She dumped the powdered orange drink mix into a bottle of water and shook it up, then dropped the packages of rice and enchiladas into the heating bag, setting it aside to warm. She ripped open the chocolate chip cookies and ate them first before tossing the squishy pouch of jalapeno-flavored cheese spread back into the bag. "Can't stand that stuff. It smells like ass and tastes even worse."

"Maybe if you read something besides Bon Appetit when we were in the field you wouldn't be so disappointed in your meal every time." He happily dumped an entire bag of Skittles into his mouth and chewed with mirth in his eyes.

"Look who's talking. Maybe you could learn something useful in that issue of Better Homes & Gardens and make this hide a little more comfortable."

"It's not my fault you wouldn't let me pack in some gardenias and a throw pillow," he said in all seriousness.

After they'd finished their meal, the duo tucked back in to their hide and waited for the patrol to pass before resuming their watch. Four hours had passed before several trucks entered the village. Soldiers spread out and began setting up camp. "Increased activity. Looks promising for our guy," Marcus said.

"I don't see him, though, do you?"

"Negative." Fedora was called such because, unlike the military garb or kaffiyeh headscarf that was normally worn, he favored a white Panama style fedora hat and a business suit.

"See if you can reach the other teams. Maybe they've spotted him."

Marcus put down his high-powered monocular and picked up the radio. After several minutes of trying, he gave up. "Still can't reach anyone. The hills are interfering with the signal. Do you want me to move to higher ground?"

"No. I'm pretty sure we have best eyes on. If he's not there, he's not there."

Early the next day, Seven and Marcus watched as more trucks arrived. There was still no sign of Fedora, but both noticed the men had brought two children with them. They were lowered from the last truck and taken to a building near the sniper team's position.

"What do you make of that?" Marcus asked.

"Good news and bad. The people of the village don't appear to be in any danger, so I'm thinking they're supporters. The arrival of the kids means it's likely we're on the right track and our guy is on the way. Since there are only two, the bastard is probably wreaking havoc nearby and will be bringing more with him when he comes."

"If he does, we have to call it in. No way they'll send in the strike if it's full of kids. Maybe we'll get lucky and he'll be using this place as his base of operation and hasn't started yet."

"Maybe."

Seven watched through her scope as a side door on the building nearest them opened and a small brown head poked out and looked around. Seeing the coast was clear, the little girl stepped out and her small companion quickly followed. She couldn't have been more than seven or eight, and the boy a year or so younger. The pair raced around to the back of the dwelling and began to play a game of some sort involving stones.

Seven was captivated. It never ceased to amaze her how children could cope with bad situations and their spirits remained intact. They didn't laugh or make any noise that she could see, but somehow they still managed to have a little fun. The girl stood with her fists planted firmly on her hips, commanding the boy to run this way and that. After a while of this exhausting enterprise, the children sat cross-legged in the dirt and she began telling him a story. Her hands gesticulated as she was making an important point and the boy seemed enthralled.

As the hours passed to days, Seven became obsessed with watching the little girl. So far, their mission had been routine reconnaissance and Fedora had not shown up. A soldier patrolled near where they were hiding several times a day, but his schedule was predictable and they were prepared when he was near.

"Sev."

"Hmm?"

"You need to take a break and rest your eyes. You've been watching those kids for hours. Come on, it's time to eat. I'll even let you choose this time." Marcus retrieved two brown MRE pouches from his pack. "Ah, delightful. For your dining pleasure this evening, we have Meal Number Twenty, Spaghetti with Meat Sauce, finely herbed, mama's own recipe with your choice of

freshly shaved parmesan or asiago cheese and a nice glass of chianti. Or, Meal Number Fourteen, Cheese Tortellini, featuring a gourmet blend of Italian cheeses in hand made pasta with a chilled glass of pinot grigio."

Seven looked over her shoulder and rolled her eyes at her partner. She turned around and settled in to take a break, grabbing the ugly brown pouch containing the tortellini as she sat. Disengaging the food from its thorough packing often took longer than eating the meal. As was her usual habit, Seven ate the dessert while her pasta was warming in its little green pouch. Her mind drifted back to the girl.

"So what is it?" Marcus asked.

"A brownie."

Marcus rolled his eyes. "I meant the kids. I've never seen you so focused on anyone before. You can't stop watching them."

Seven took a swig of her orange drink, downing half the bottle in a few giant gulps. "I don't know exactly. I'm not really the sentimental type, but watching them has made me miss home."

After the Marines finished up the last of their meals, Seven turned back to her scope and quickly found the children as Marcus settled beside her. She smiled and laughed quietly as the girl attempted to spin the little boy around her and they both fell in a laughing heap.

"What's so funny?" Marcus asked, turning toward the village.

"Jenny used to do that with her little brother," Seven said without thinking. She looked up and smiled. "It just hit me why she reminds me of home. She's a lot like someone I used to know when I was a kid. It was a long time ago, but they were good memories. Jenny

always made up stories and games like that little girl down there."

Just then, a commotion broke out in the village. Hearing the noise, the kids quickly scrambled back inside. Marcus was the first to spot him. "Target at ten o'clock," he said, causing Seven to swing her rifle scope to the directed area.

"Son of a bitch, that's him. Like a peacock preening for his men. Marcus, how much trouble do you think I'd get in if I just put one between his eyes right now?" Seven asked. Their mission was only to observe and report back so command could strike the village before Fedora got away.

"We could take out the patrol, sneak down there and grab the kids, come back up here, and I could take him out before they ever knew what was happening."

"As much as I'm sure we'd both enjoy that, you know we can't. What if there are guards with the kids? What if we terrified the kids and they started screaming? They'd swarm the hills looking for us and it would put us and the other teams in danger."

"I know. I know, but damn. This is one kill I sure wouldn't lose any sleep over."

"It's not our job, this time."

Fedora gave a cursory glance around the village then pointed to a building on the northern side. His men quickly began unloading gear bags and boxes from his trucks and took them to where he'd indicated.

"He didn't bring any kids with him this time. This is good news. We need to report back immediately before he gets to work."

"Roger that. Move up to high ground and radio in what we've seen. Tell them about the kids and see if they'll change our directive. I want them out of there

before they hit it."

Seven resumed her watch on Fedora. It would be so easy. He was in her crosshairs. She made a slight adjustment to her scope, breathing slowly in through her mouth and out through her nose. A trickle of sweat ran down her neck, distracting her from the smooth metal of the trigger against her fingertip. All she had to do was apply a little pressure and it would all be over.

Fedora was giving a rallying speech to his troops, waving a rifle around and punctuating his statements by jabbing it in the air. She couldn't hear what he was saying, but it was obvious by the rapt attention and shouts from his followers that his point was being well made. Her eyes were drawn to the men standing behind him who, unlike the others, all seemed quite bored with the proceedings.

It wasn't a conscious thought, but something about them wasn't right. She moved the scope from face to face taking in their appearance. Same age, weight, height, coloring, facial hair - the similarities in the five men to Fedora wasn't just uncanny, it was unnatural.

Fedora finished his speech as his men howled and shot their rifles in the air. Just at that moment, he glanced over his shoulder to one of the doppelgangers to his right. He was dressed more traditionally, like the others, but wore a white kaffiyeh with a black agal. He gave a subtle nod of approval, then his eyes went back to scanning the crowd and hills beyond.

"Son of a bitch," Seven whispered to herself. "The bastard is using a decoy." She heard a rustle in the bushes behind her and turned quickly to see Marcus coming in. Seven turned back to her scope and zeroed in on the man she now knew to be the real Fedora. He and two others got into one of the trucks and drove out of the

northern end of the village.

"God damn it!" She hissed through her teeth.

"Pack it up, Sev. Our orders are to move to the extract point ASAP. The strike is coming in."

"No! Marcus, it's not him!"

"What? What do you mean, it's not him? I can see him down there with my bare eyes."

"That guy is a decoy. The real one just left the village in an armored truck. We've got to get back and call off the strike," she said urgently. "Those kids are still in there!"

"You know as well as I do they're not going to miss the opportunity to wipe him out because of two kids. Thirty, yes. Two, no way. He's a high-priority target."

"Marcus, think about it. It's not him! That's why the guy always wears the distinctive clothing. That's why the SEAL ops thought they had him twice but missed. He's been doing this all along."

"It's out of our hands. All we can do is radio the info to command, but either way, we need to get the hell out of here right now. We are way too close." Marcus grabbed Seven by the collar and tugged. "Seven, now!"

Seven's body felt like a bowstring pulled tight, her will ready to release like a deadly arrow on the village. It was the fear in her best friend's voice that snapped her back to reality.

She felt helpless. She looked back at the building that held the little girl one last time before grabbing her gear and running as fast as her legs would carry her toward the hilltop, and hopefully a decent radio signal.

They found the two other sniper teams waiting for them at the rally point. Marcus quickly dropped his pack and pulled the radio gear out. "Command, this is team Alpha, do you read?"

"Affirmative, team Alpha. Go ahead."

"Target has left the area. I repeat, target has left the area. Proceeding north in armored vehicle."

The other Marines looked at him questioningly. Last they knew, Fedora was definitely there.

"Acknowledged, message received. Proceed to evac immediately, Tomahawks inbound."

Seven and Marcus made eye contact and silently accepted that there was nothing else they could do.

Later the next day, Seven sat at a small wooden desk in a tent she shared with five other women. She didn't sleep at all, visions of the small black haired girl playing like a movie in her head. She pulled a piece of paper from the desk, put a date at the top, and began writing.

Dear Jenny,

I'm sorry it's been so long since I've written, but something happened this week that has me missing you terribly and the simpler days when we were close. I can't help but wonder if your tenacious spirit and creative endeavors followed you into adulthood. I'm sure you won't be surprised when I tell you I joined the Marines, like my dad. You always said

One of her bunkmates came up behind her. "Michelis, Sergeant Johnson to see you outside."

Marcus was waiting for her as she exited the tent. "Hi."

"Hi."

"You okay?"

Seven nodded. She was taking this one hard and he knew it.

"Thought you'd like to know. The Lieutenant said that after we'd called in about Fedora, they were able to track the truck via satellite. They took it out. They got him, Seven."

"Any news on the village? Survivors?"

"No word on that yet, but you know there's always a chance she made it. The missile was targeted to the northern part of the village so it's possible she survived."

"Michelis, Johnson, round up your team, pack your gear, and get to the hangar. We're shipping out in thirty minutes." Their commander barked from some distance away.

"Where to now?" Marcus wondered aloud.

"Don't know but we better hustle." Seven returned to her tent and made quick work of stowing her personal items before heading back out into the dry heat of another stifling day. Her letter to Jenny was forgotten.

Jenny got up from her warm spot on the couch and walked naked over to the bar, retrieving a decanter of scotch and two tumblers. She returned to the couch, poured them each a glass, and settled back under the blanket, reclaiming her spot and taking Seven into her arms.

"Did you ever find out what happened to the girl?" she asked.

"No. We were long gone before any news came in. I hope she made it though. It tore me up inside for a long time, not knowing."

Seven took a long drink from her glass and cringed slightly. "I don't know what I'm going to do without him, Jen. My heart hurts when I think about what I lost. He saved me from myself that day. I was thinking with my heart and not my head, and soldiers die when that happens." She closed her eyes as if she could block out the thoughts, then whispered, "I put the entire mission in jeopardy. He kept me on track; otherwise I probably would have gone off half-cocked and gotten us all killed."

Jenny set her glass down and wrapped Seven in a tender hug. "You loved him. From everything you've told me about him, he loved you too."

"I can't help but think that his death was my fault, somehow. Logically, I know it wasn't, but he wouldn't have even been in Bolivia if it weren't for me." Tears began to flow freely down Seven's cheeks. Her voice shook as she said, "I was so selfish. I wanted him with me when I left the Marines. I couldn't save him. I couldn't protect him. I couldn't save or protect that little girl, either."

"Shhh, shhh, baby, it's all right. You can't do this to yourself. You did everything you could for both of them." Jenny faced her fully and reached up to wipe the tears from her face tenderly.

"But what if I can't protect you either? What if something happens to you and I'm helpless?" She began to cry in earnest.

Jenny had never seen her lover so despondent. She felt Seven's grief like a kick in the stomach and her eyes began to well from the invisible pain. She had noticed changes in Seven's behavior in the last few weeks, but it wasn't until right now that she realized the depth of her sadness. All she wanted in the world was to take away her suffering. She searched frantically within herself for the right words to say. "Seven, listen to me." Jenny held her face gently. She retrieved her t-shirt from the floor and used it to dry Seven's eyes. "I can take care of myself, and you know what? I can take care of you too. Maybe just this once you can let it be me that does the protecting?"

Seven seemed to melt into Jenny's secure embrace. Jenny knew in her heart that her lover would not let this inner turmoil get the best of her.

"I think maybe I need to see someone, Jen," she whispered quietly.

Jenny stroked her hair as she held her close. "I think so, too. Don't worry, baby, we'll get through this together. Whatever you need, I love you, and I'm here for you, okay?"

Seven nodded, grateful for the loving shoulder she had to cry on.

❧❧❧❧

It was late afternoon and Seven was sitting on the tiny back porch of their townhome, absently strumming the chords of a Chrissie Hynde song on her dad's old six string. She found that plucking the well-worn guitar was a great stress reliever. She quietly sang a slow, melodic version of the song 'Kid', the haunting lyrics seeming to fit her mood.

It had been a few weeks since Seven proposed to Jenny. That day had been a strange turning point for Seven in more ways than one. Not only had she committed to love Jenny for the rest of her life, but she had finally come to terms with her need for a therapist to overcome the swirling emotions she felt over the death of her friend.

Her first appointment with the doctor was tomorrow. She was nervous, but at the same time, she felt lighter somehow just knowing she was taking a step in the right direction.

She couldn't see much of the sky from her position, but Seven figured she would have to move inside soon. The wind was picking up and the air seemed to darken around her.

She kicked her feet up onto the railing and shivered a little as a gust of cool wind blew up her pant leg. She wished Jenny were home. The young woman had left several hours ago, needing to drive into the city for something. It seemed like they hadn't been separated for more than a few minutes since Jenny had dug her out of a hole in the deep Bolivian woods all those months ago. She wondered on some level if Jenny would still love her, knowing she was damaged goods.

Seven quickly disregarded the self-depreciating thought. The one thing she did know for sure right now was that Jenny loved her. She thanked the fates for her good fortune.

"That's such a beautiful song," Jenny's soft voice came through the screen door. "I love it when you sing."

Seven turned and smiled at the welcome intrusion. Relief washed over her at seeing her lover returned from the city safe and sound. She stood and made her way to the door, which squeaked on its hinges as it was pushed open for her to enter. She noticed immediately that Jenny was looking at her like a hungry predator looks at a future meal. Jenny took the guitar from her hand and set it on the floor by the back door.

"Missed you," Seven said.

There was no mistaking the younger woman's mood or intention as she slid her hands behind Seven's neck and pulled her down for a deep and very erotic kiss. Seven's knees shook and her heart rate began to pound as Jenny's tongue traced her lips then delved into her mouth. It amazed her how her lover could have her completely aroused in about ten seconds.

With no further words between them, Jenny took Seven by the hand and led her to the living room. Their lips never parted as she gently pushed her down into the leather armchair and straddled her lap.

"Guess you missed me too," Seven panted, her libido now out of her control.

Jenny's hands moved between them and worked to unbutton the soft old oxford Seven wore over her braless torso. She pushed the fabric aside, her lips following her fingertips as she left a trail of kisses along the same path. Seven immediately missed the warmth and weight as Jenny slid off her lap and dropped to the floor between her knees. The first button on her favorite pair of threadbare Levi's was pulled open at the same moment warm lips enclosed her nipple.

Seven's head fell to the back of the chair, her breathing coming louder and faster. "Jesus," she panted. "Remind me to sing more often." A jolt of pure pleasure electrified her senses.

"Lift."

Seven raised her hips and watched as her jeans and panties were pulled over her hips, slowly down her legs and off, landing in a heap nearby. Jenny's smoldering eyes never left hers as her strong hands kneaded the muscles in her calves and thighs. She bent her head low and began leaving a trail of warm kisses from her ankles to the inside of her knees, then higher.

"Scootch forward."

Seven did as directed with no hesitation. The

warmth of the leather chair at her back, the insistent attentions of her lover in front, the scents and sounds surrounding her had her body and mind reeling. She hissed through her teeth when Jenny reached her goal. There was something so unbelievably erotic about watching her lover on her knees giving her this gift. She felt like a goddess. She felt worshipped.

Seven reached for Jenny, running her fingers through her soft hair. She wanted to throw her head back, close her eyes, and ride the sensation, but at the same time she couldn't take her eyes off her lover. It was an internal battle until at last she could hold on no longer. Her white knuckled fingers dug into the warm leather of the armrests, she threw her head back and gasped as her whole body began to spasm.

When she could open her eyes again, she looked at Jenny, who seemed quite pleased with herself. Her lover crawled into her lap and flung her legs over the arm of the chair, burying her face in Seven's neck and holding her close. They simply sat and held each other for a time while Seven's heart rate returned to its normal state.

Finally, Jenny said, "Yes, I missed you too."

Seven chuckled, causing the blonde bundle in her lap to bounce. "I could tell."

"I was thinking about you a lot today, because I was on a very special errand. I was trying to come up with a creative way to present this to you, but everything I thought of failed in comparison to a proposal while jumping out of a plane." Jenny reached into her pocket and took out a small, deep blue velvet pouch. She opened it and withdrew a dazzling three-eighths inch band of gold inlaid with a single row of square cut emeralds. It was very contemporary in its design, but classic all the same.

Seven was speechless. She stared at the stunning ring and numbly held out her hand for Jenny to put it on. The oversized width of the band looked beautiful on her long fingers, the yellow gold a perfect complement to her skin tone. "Oh my god, Jen," she whispered. "I don't know what to say…it's…it's…"

"It's you." Jenny smiled sweetly.

"The emeralds are the same color as your eyes." She captured Jenny's lips in a tender kiss.

"I had it custom made. I wanted to give you something unique, like you are. The emeralds are to remind you of me. As long as you wear that ring, you will have me with you."

"That is so sweet."

"There's something else too."

Seven looked up expectantly.

"The gold belonged to Marcus. I wanted you to have something to remember him by always. I wanted you to know that the people who love you will always watch over you."

"But wha…how…?"

"I asked his mother if she had any keepsake of his I could give you as a remembrance. I didn't know what she would send, but when I got his class ring in the mail, I knew it was meant to be. I had it made into this band so you would have a piece of him with you always."

Seven stroked the warm metal with her thumb. The sentiment behind Jenny's actions was selfless and a little overwhelming. "I wish you'd known him. He would have loved you."

"I'm yours forever, Seven. I will always be here for you. Together we can dodge bullets, jump from airplanes, conquer this, and anything else that comes our way. I can't even begin to tell you how much I am looking forward to our life together."

Seven squeezed her tight. For the first time in weeks, she felt her inner turmoil calm. Jenny was right. As long as they had each other, she could jump and no matter how hard the fall, she would always have a soft landing.

Lesley is originally from Michigan, spent her college years in Texas, and now lives in Florida with her partner of 27 years, along with Biscuit, the crazy Westie. A degree in journalism led to a career as a copywriter and creative director in the advertising and marketing industry. Leslie's debut novel Sharpshooter won a Goldie in 2015.

Asher

By Shannon M. Harris

One hundred and forty years before The Festival of the
Goddess
Deplire, Candor

Asher waited as patiently as she could outside the Guild Master's office door, her breathing in sync with the tapping of her foot. From an early age everyone told her she was special and now that she allowed her specialness to shine through, she was being punished for it. She couldn't help the fact that everyone's magic, compared to hers, was subpar. She sighed and pushed away from the wall, looked at the shut door and started pacing. The red band on her wrist taunted her. She should be allowed some lenience because of her status, but knew that wouldn't be the case. The higher the band you received the more responsibilities that were placed on you. She quickly retook her seat when the door opened and one of her classmates walked out.

"He'll see you know," he said smirking and walking away.

Great. She was condemned even before she uttered a single word. She stood, nodded at the guard by the door and entered the room. She wouldn't go down without a fight and she would be damned if they stripped her of any of her bands. Without looking at anything in the room she bowed her head out of respect for the Guild Master only to lock eyes with the Queen of Candor. Quickly lowering herself to one knee, she bowed before her. This was more serious then she first thought. For the Queen to be present only meant one thing: trouble. She was in deep trouble. Rising only when the Queen instructed her to, she sank into one of the chairs in front of the desk and for the first time noticed the Guild Master seated in a chair by the window. The frown on his face spoke volumes about his mood. Out of respect, Asher bowed her head in his direction then turned her full attention on the Queen. She was beautiful in an untouchable sort of way. Her long, curly black hair was pulled back from her face and her green eyes held a depth Asher had never seen before.

Queen Laurel cocked her head and spoke. "I hear there has been some trouble of late where you are concerned, Asher. Tell me about it." There wasn't any malice in her voice, just curiosity.

"Majesty, if I may," the Guild Master cut in.

"You may not," Laurel said, never taking her eyes off of Asher.

Asher sighed and counted to ten before speaking. "I'm not sure where to start." She ran her hands through her short white hair, which left it standing at odd angles all over her head. That was one of the reasons everyone treated her differently, because she looked different than the majority of Candor's citizens. She didn't realize when she was transferred from Falnor to Deplire that she would face the kind of backlash from her fellow classmates that she had thus far received.

"I've always found the beginning a good choice," The Queen said. "I believe there was an incident involving a deer." She arched her eyebrow.

Asher laughed then shut up when the Guild Master glared at her. "Yes, the deer." She nodded seriously. "That was entirely my fault. I didn't want to go on the hunting trip but they told me it was my duty." She shook her head. "I don't find joy in killing innocent creatures but they insisted. We walked all day and didn't have any luck. Everyone decided to call it quits for the day when we spotted a small buck grazing in the field below us. They were all being so callus about this creature's life that I got a little upset. I told them that the least they could do was say a prayer before they killed him but they laughed at me." She locked her sky blue eyes with the Queen's. "I don't like being laughed at. When they readied their arrows I walked in front of them and into the valley. When I heard an arrow coming at me I grabbed it out of the air and threw it back at them." She blew out a breath and shrugged. "I didn't know I could throw something that far and have it be that accurate with my bare hands. It even impressed me."

"The arrow pierced one man's shoulder and went clean through striking the man behind him. How did you do it? What spell did you use?" The Queen leaned forward.

"I didn't use a spell or at least not one consciously and to be fair I didn't hit my mark." She bit her lip. "I aimed for his heart."

"You missed your mark." The Queen shook her head. "Let's all be glad you did because if you had hit it you would already have been put to death. Using your magic in such a way goes against everything you were taught. But to be fair," she said glancing at the Guild Master. "When she stepped in front of them, everyone on that hill should have never fired an arrow."

"You believe her?" He stammered.

"Why are you so quick to dismiss her words, but not those of the others?" She turned back to Asher. "I believe there was another incident yesterday."

Oh, boy. She wouldn't be able to get out of this one. "I have no excuse and no real explanation for what occurred yesterday only to say that it wasn't my intention for any of it to happen. I admit to causing the collapse in the library and I admit freely to the carnage in the kitchen. When it happens, it happens so fast sometimes I don't have time to react or control the emotions that well up inside me. It's frustrating," she said standing and running her hands through her hair before taking up position behind her chair. "I will take my punishment with an open and willing heart." She grimaced when the Queen stood, walked around the desk and leaned back against it crossing her arms across her perfectly tailored green blouse. She was every bit a Queen and even though she shouldn't have, Asher couldn't help but wonder how she kept her white trousers so clean.

"You're a red band sorceress," the Queen said bringing Asher back to reality. "If I may. You should have never made it this far if your emotions colored your control over your magic. So how did you?"

"She's good at deception." The Guild Master also stood and walked toward them but when the Queen held out her hand her guard intercepted him and showed him back to his seat.

"To tell you the truth before being assigned here I didn't have any trouble controlling my emotions. At every turn here someone is trying to goad me or taunt me or something," she said waving her hands. "I know I shouldn't let it get to me but at every other place I was stationed everyone looked out for each other." She shook her head and started pacing. "I know I'm different. The hair, the eyes, the accent. I hear it every day and you know what?" She stopped pacing and looked back at the Queen.

"What?" Laurel said pushing away from the desk.

"It gets old after a while. I'm a very good sorceress and I may not be what everyone here thinks I should be but I am me and I think I am pretty remarkable." She couldn't believe she had spoken to the Queen in such a manner and an instant later she regretted it. "I'm sorry my Queen. You're not my enemy." She felt defeated. After everything they would win.

"You know what, Asher. I hear your frustration and I can see your frustration. What I want to know is why didn't you ask to be assigned to another post? You can ask to be transferred somewhere else if the reason," the Queen said, "is within reason."

"I did." Asher shrugged. "My Guild Master," she said pointing at him. "Told me that in order to be allowed to leave I would have to get my emotions under control but I don't see how I can do that here. I'm a prisoner."

The Queen looked toward the Guild Master then back to Asher. Walking around the desk she retook her seat, picked up a piece of paper and started to write. When she finished she told Asher to sit. "When my advisories informed me of this situation I couldn't help but be intrigued and since I was already in the city I took it upon myself to personally deal with it. I'm not sure how it could not have occurred to everyone that you don't belong here. You may have the abilities of a One sorceress but you are not a One Sorceress. You may have the abilities of an Item Sorceress but you are not an Item Sorceress. I believe, my dear, you are both and possibly more. In all of my sixties years I have never encountered someone quite like you. As rare as that is, someone messed up badly when they placed you here but I don't think it was intentional. What I do know is that not being allowed to leave was intentional. Since both men were completely healed from your arrow attack and no harm really occurred in the kitchen and the library I see no reason to punish you further. But in the future that may not be the case. Besides," she winked, "The book shelves in the library needed to be replaced anyway. As for your next placement I don't see any reason why you can't pick your own. You have a few choices."

"Wait a minute," The Guild Master said. "She's going to get away with what she's done."

"Sit down, Aaron. I will deal with you later. Not one more outburst." She never once glanced his way.

Asher happily kept quiet but didn't fully understand what had just occurred. How could she be both a One Sorceress and an Item Sorceress or more? Did it mean she could do any kind of magic she wanted? That would be awesome. And why was the Queen letting her get away with what had occurred. None of it made any sense, but she would not be the one to question it.

"Like I was saying before being interrupted. You have a few choices. You can be stationed here in Candor, at a different location of course. You can choose to go back to Manight, Malora or if you're really looking for an adventure you can choose Laramore. I will give you some time to choose."

"Actually," Asher said. "I don't need any time. I would like to be stationed in Malora." She heard they were doing great things and would love to learn from their healers.

The Queen only hesitated briefly before answering. "Very well. Whenever you're ready I will have someone escort you there and I will inform the Guild Master that you're on your way." She started to stand then sat back down. "If I may ask, why Malora?"

"Why not." Asher smiled with more confidence than she felt. "Besides, I've always wanted to learn healing more in-depth and where else to learn except from the best. This will grant me an opportunity I wouldn't have otherwise been afforded." For the first time in a long time she didn't dread the future, but was looking forward to it.

"I believe we're done here. You will leave day after tomorrow."

"Thank you, Your Highness."

❧❦❧❦

The trip to Malora took longer than Asher thought possible. She finally arrived three days ago and so far everyone treated her, dare she say, nice. She didn't know if they knew her circumstances but if they did they didn't let on and for that she would be forever grateful. She resided in one of the housing units off campus for the simple fact that she wasn't a healer bound sorceress by birth. The small building they assigned her to housed twenty other students and each one had their own room. Each room held a bed, a small table and enough space for her to store all of her belongings. Today was her first full day of studies and everything fascinated her. The idea of healing someone stoked the very core of her being. Some classes she knew would be more challenging than others but hard work never slowed her down.

When classes ended for the day she was both excited and a little disappointed. She had the next two days to rest before her first full week of classes started the following week and she couldn't wait to explore the city. She knew it was a step back from where she came from and a few of her fellow students couldn't believe that she had already received her red band because some of her teachers didn't even have theirs yet. She was only one step away from being a white band sorceress but coming here she essentially started over. It scared her knowing that all her previous teaching wouldn't necessarily help her but a fresh start was exactly what she needed after everything that happened in Deplire.

After dropping her bag off at her room she headed toward the marketplace. Malora's system of governing would take some getting used to. They didn't deal in money. Everyone did their job and everyone's needs were taking care of. When she first arrived in the city she was fitted with a leather bracelet that molded to her skin. It allowed all the merchants to recognize her as a student of healing. As such, she would receive anything she needed free and in exchange she signed a contract stating that she would dedicate two years of her life to the healing needs of Malora after her studies were completed. She didn't have a problem with that but made herself a promise not to take advantage of anyone's generosity.

She walked among the vendors in the marketplace, taking in every detail. It was all so different from

Candor and she liked it that way. Sameness was boring. She stopped, closed her eyes and inhaled deeply. The Ocean smelled different here. Somehow cleaner. The bread and roasting nuts invaded her senses bringing a smile to her face and made her stomach grumble. She opened her eyes only to close them a moment later. After a few seconds she opened one eye, then the other, just to make sure the woman buying bread at the vendor ahead of her was real. The woman, who looked to be around her age, wore a long, blue and brown fitted dress and her curly brown hair was pulled up on her neck. When she turned Asher got a good look at her face and her pulse quickened when she saw the woman's smile and dimples. Heart pounding she made her way closer and stopped beside the stall. She didn't know if it was the woman or the baking bread but something smelled amazing. When the woman turned to leave, Asher purposely stepped aside so she would run into her.

"Oh," the woman said smiling and holding onto Asher's arm. "I'm sorry. Pardon me."

"Not a problem." When she didn't say anything else and the woman stepped away she felt like kicking herself. How could she let her leave? Why didn't she say something? She frowned then turned toward the vendor who was smirking at her. "What?" she said a little louder then she intended to and stuffed her hands in her pockets.

He held his hands up and backed away, but he was smiling. "Missed opportunity if I ever did see one." He chuckled.

"You think?" She bit her lip.

He nodded. "I do." He cocked his head and regarded her seriously. "Are you going to stand here or are you going after her." He pointed to where the woman stood a good ways down looking at fabric. Asher didn't think she stood a chance but coming here was all about second chances and in the worst case scenario she would say no. She could handle a no. Maybe.

"I am but first can I get one of those cinnamon rolls. They smell really good." She let him see her bracelet and he handed over the roll, his eyes growing wide when he saw her red band. "Nothing to worry about. This," she said pointing at her band. "This is the past and this place is my new beginning."

"Good." He nodded then seemed to make up his mind. "Every now and then we could all use a change. Oh," he called after her, "her name is Becky." She thanked him and stepped away taking a large bite of the roll. The flavors were amazing and she would make it a point to visit his stall at least once a day. As she got closer to Becky she seemed to have more of a bounce in her step. Rejection would suck but not even asking for a chance would suck even more. She stepped behind Becky and waited in line. They were at another fabric vendor. That reminded her that she would need to see a tailor soon. When Becky stepped up Asher was so lost in her thoughts that she didn't hear the vendor address her. "I'm sorry. What?" She said looking around.

"I said, can I be of any help to you today." The vendor was a much older woman and she didn't look all that friendly but Asher knew from experience looks could be deceiving. She looked between Becky and the Vendor then at Becky's arms, which were empty.

"I'm confused," she said, rocking back on her heals. "Has Becky been waited on yet?" Becky grinned and looked back toward the vendor.

"No. I saw your bracelet and wondered if I could get anything for you. Seeing as how you're busy and all."

Asher decided she wouldn't be coming back to this stall. "I don't see how my red band should put me above her or anyone else. She should have been waited on before me."

The vendor shrugged. "Your wrong, but I'll let it go." She turned to Becky. "Can I help you?"

"No, not today," Becky said walking off.

"Very well," the vendor said. "Next."

It took Asher a minute to catch up with her because she was walking so fast. "Becky," Asher called out to get her attention. "Why the getaway?" She laughed.

"I wanted to see how far you would follow me?" She said it with a straight face but Asher could see the mischief behind her deep brown eyes.

"I would have followed you wherever you went." She noticed for the first time that Becky stood a good few inches taller than her.

"Is that so?"

"It is." She held out her hand. "I'm Asher."

"That's a unique name," Becky said letting go of her hand. "You seem to already know mine."

Asher bit her lip. "The cinnamon roll vendor told me."

Becky nodded then smirked. "He's my uncle."

Figured. "So I was wondering if you've eaten yet. Maybe we could have lunch together," She stammered.

"In fact I haven't." Becky smiled.

When she didn't elaborate Asher asked, "So is that a yes you will have lunch with me, or no I'm not your type." Asher held her breath when Becky reached toward her and smoothed her finger across her upper lip.

"You had a little sugar left over from the roll," she said in answer to Asher's question. "And yes I will have lunch with you. But for the record, I'm not easy and I expect to be courted properly."

Asher crossed her arms. "I don't have a problem with that. In fact that's what I prefer." She led the way to the Inn and sat across from Becky when the waitress seated them.

"So," Becky said after they had eaten. "What brings you here, to Malora?" She cut her eyes to Asher's red band.

"I was stationed in Candor but during my last assignment there was a bit of trouble so I was allowed to pick where my next placement would be. Queen Laurel didn't have to give me the choice and I will forever be grateful that she did." Asher traced the red band tattooed around her wrist and locked onto Becky's eyes. "I am a red band sorceress. I was misdiagnosed from the beginning and for that reason my placement was wrong. I am a One sorceress and an Item sorceress and maybe more. I don't know exactly what that means, but I can't wait to find out. It's scary and exciting at the same time."

"So you're searching for something?"

"Not searching, exactly. More like experimenting. I don't know everything I am capable of, but I know I want to do something centered on medicine and healing. That's why I'm here."

Becky picked up her glass and looked at Asher over the rim. "Won't your studies take up most of your time?"

Asher waited until she set the glass down before answering. "I think," she said grasping Becky's hand

and tracing the lines on her palm, "that I will have plenty of time to explore much more than my studies."

"Really." Becky pulled her hand away, bit her lip and seemed to be searching for something. "You should know I don't come from a fancy background. My mother died when I was young and my father has worked as a fisherman his whole life. What in the world could someone of your status possibly see in me?"

"I don't come from a fancy background either. I was just lucky enough to be blessed with Goddess Shara's gifts. I don't care about your status and I know we just met, but I think we should give this a go." She ran her hands through her hair, leaving it sticking up in several places. "I like you and I think this could be something special if you will give me a chance." Before Asher could say anything Becky stood up and headed for the door. How in the world had she already blown it in so little time? It had to have been a record.

"Asher," Becky called out.

Asher took a second to regain her composure, vowing she would not make a fool of herself in front of Becky or the other patrons of the Inn. Everyone had the right their own choices and she would have to accept Becky's. Slowly standing she found the courage to turn and face her and the smile on Becky's face was almost her undoing. "Yes."

Becky smirked and pointed to the marketplace. "Let's get out of here."

"Are you sure?" She asked the question not sure she wanted the answer, but she had to know.

"Yes. I am sure."

"Fair enough," Asher whispered and followed Becky out the door, but instead of heading toward the temples Becky turned in the opposite direction. Asher grinned but kept her cool when Becky reached out and grasped her hand. After a short but pleasant walk they left behind the bustling city center and Becky turned left toward the ocean. She zigzagged so much through the streets and alleyways that Asher knew she would never be able to find her way back to the university by herself.

"Okay," Becky said and pulled Asher to a stop near, what looked to be, an overgrown and deserted property. The hedges that lined the area in front of them were at least ten feet tall and had vines and some type of berry growing all over them. "Not many people still visit here, but I love to. It's so peaceful and I feel such comfort and love that I can stay here for hours. I know you're not from around here so I will give you a bit of a history lesson."

Asher nodded. "I like history."

"Good. How much do you know about Goddess Nia?"

Asher curled her fingers around Becky's and took a moment to answer. "I know what I read in all the history books available to me. I don't worship her, but I respect her stance and I respect everything she has to offer to her followers."

Becky pulled her hand away, walked to the vine covered wall and leaned against it. "So not much." She laughed. "Nia is known for being simplistic in nature and for the record, so am I. She doesn't believe in flaunting ones wealth or power and she definitely doesn't believe in competing with others to prove your worth."

"You talk about here like she's still here."

"That's because she is. She is with us always."

No one she knew talked of Shara in such a

manner and neither did she. If people asked she would tell them she was a follower of Shara, but she wouldn't call herself devout. The love for Nia radiated off Becky. "That's a refreshing change to the followers of Shara."

"I guess it would be a big difference. They are both so different. I don't dislike or disrespect the other gods, I just know for me there will only be Nia." She pointed to her right and pushed off the wall. "When Nia still walked these streets someone created this place as a sanctuary, not only for her but for any weary soul that followed her. No one knows who the person was because he or she wanted to remain anonymous. I know it doesn't look like much from the outside, but wait until you enter." She grabbed Asher's hand and walked a few feet down from where they stood and when she found what she was looking for she walked through the vines. Asher threw her hand up to keep the vines from falling in her face and stopped when she got her first look at their surroundings. A simple, wooden alter set in the middle of a small garden, surrounded at the base with brown and red striped pillows. In all four corners benches had been placed and from the looks of the wood, they had to have been there for quite some time. The roof of the garden was made up of long, slender trees that were covered in moss and several different types of mushrooms. There was at least two feet of distance in-between each tree to allow sunlight to shine through. Brightly colored flowers raced up the walls and collided with each other to create a vibrant picture that could have only been created by a master gardener. She inhaled deeply and closed her eyes as the sweet smell of honeysuckle assaulted her senses. After several minutes she opened her eyes and grinned. She didn't know what it was, but

Becky was right, this place had a calming effort. "This place is magical." Still holding tightly to Becky's hand she walked to a bench in the far corner and sat down pulling Becky down beside her.

Becky leaned back and into Asher. "It is magical. I don't know why more people don't visit."

"Who knows? The gardener must be very skilled to create such a work of art and to keep it this way?"

Becky bit her lip and stood up. "There is no gardener. This is the way it has looked for thousands of years. No one takes care of this place. It takes care of itself."

Asher swung her gaze around the garden then stood up and ran her fingers along the flowers on the wall. "How is that possible?" She knew magic could create amazing things, but to sustain this type of illusion was breathtaking. Everything looked so real. The smell, the colors and the weathered wood on the benches was incredible. She was wrong, a master gardener didn't create this place, a master sorcerer did. She walked around the garden inspecting everything she could get her hands on and looking for any crack in the armor. After a few passes around she couldn't find any. This is what she wanted to accomplish. An illusion that would stand the test of time. "I am speechless. What a gift someone has given you."

"It truly is a gift." By this time Becky had returned to the bench. She patted the spot beside her and without a second thought Asher sat down next to her.

"Thank you. Seeing this place has only solidified, for me, that I am in the right place. Maybe all these years it hasn't been Shara guiding me, maybe it's been Nia."

"Nia has a way of showing us what we never

thought possible and bringing people into our lives at just the right time. Whether we think it is or not. Her fate for us is already set. I wasn't looking for anyone but our plans are not her plans."

This certainly was a complete change in direction for her. When she arrived a few days ago the only relationship she expected to have was with her teachers. Now all that had changed. Unlike Becky, though, she didn't believe her fate was already set, but she did believe people were brought into your life to challenge and enhance it. She smiled and lifted Becky's hand to her lips and placed a tender kiss on it. Candor was an experience she would never forget and all the destruction she caused was the best thing she could have ever done. Things were certainly a lot brighter in Malora and she couldn't wait to see what the future held.

Born near Chicago, IL, but raised in Southern Illinois, Shannon is a diehard Whovian and enjoys anything having to do with Science Fiction and Fantasy. In her free time, when she isn't writing, she enjoys binge watching true crime shows. She lives in the country with her three fur kids.

On Peculiar Ground

By S.Y. Thompson

I'm here," Leena Kyle spoke into the headset. "I don't see her. Are you sure these are the right coordinates?"

A male voice responded through the communications static. Even inside her full-face helmet, with the roar of the wind muted, Leena could hardly make out the words. She glanced briefly back at the flyer, a vessel used for hovering above a planet's surface. It stood out gunmetal dark against the frozen tundra and Leena knew it wouldn't be long before she couldn't spot the vehicle in the storm.

"Her tracker is there...sure of it."

Leena grimaced. Everyone from the Cities Alliance had trackers injected at birth. Still, the fact that the beacon registered as nearby didn't really mean anything. Someone, or something, could have cut it out of Andera Sol's skin. Leena didn't want to consider the possibility, so she tried to force it from her mind. Instead, she concentrated on searching, a task made more difficult by current conditions.

Wind pelted her with icy fragments. She could hear the tiny projectiles whacking the side of her helmet. Her body shivered inside the peacekeeper's uniform, though Alliance engineers designed it to provide comfort no matter what the weather. The white material blended with the blizzard. Only her elbows, knees and the piping around her helmet stood out. Black against the unfamiliar alabaster snow.

Leena took another faltering step and sank up to her hips. The heads-up display, or H.U.D., inside her helmet beeped a warning too late. Temperature readouts filled the left side of her screen. They were all in the red, much too cold for any warm-blooded humanoid. Not for the first time, she appreciated the properties of this once hated uniform. She'd sworn never to wear it again, but wasn't able to discard it completely. Ironic how that decision might save two lives today.

She strained to climb back onto the rocky ridge. Dusted with blowing snow, Leena's grasp felt all the more precarious. The wind howled and tried to push her backward into the heavy drifts. Leena persevered and managed to extricate herself from the powder. Despite the frigid planet surface, Leena's copper-colored short hair clung to her forehead and the back of her neck. Her efforts left her sweating and exhausted, but she refused to stop. Andera needed her.

An image of the diminutive scientist came to mind, causing Leena to smile. Andera's long blond hair clasped into a hasty ponytail, the dimple in her left cheek when she smiled, the way full breasts heaved when Andera took a deep breath...

"Okay, Leena, back on point. Focus. You can tell her how wonderful she is after you save her life."

As if. Leena hadn't found the courage to speak those words since meeting Andera four months ago. The quest to abandon a devastated world of doomed cities in faster than light ships hadn't afforded the opportunity. Since landing on this new planet, innocently dubbed New Horizons, Leena had used building a new society as an excuse not to interact with Andera on a more personal level. Now, she might not get another chance.

"Right, focus."

From the rocky shelf, Leena surveyed the area. Barren and stunted trees littered the landscape. Not thick or heavy enough to provide refuge, they presented a trip hazard beneath the snow. Gnarled roots and fallen branches concealed obstacles that promised to rend flesh and shatter bone. Leena hoped to avoid that particular exciting experience.

"Interface," she said to the helmet's intelli-computer, "activate boot skids."

Small, ski-like devices slid outward from the fronts and backs of Leena's boots. The contraptions curled up slightly in front. Made for water, Leena figured they would function just as well in this situation. She didn't figure the sleek bottoms of the skids into her equation. When Leena stepped back onto the snow, her right foot slid forward until she thought her crotch would split. The heavy emergency pack she carried on her back served only to throw her off balance even further. She managed to pull her left foot forward enough to save herself from painful cramps.

"Ouch," she grumbled, "I don't have time to learn how to walk again."

Leena kept her voice low, aware of Captain Chase listening on the other end. The constant squelch of static made that unlikely, but she didn't want to take any chances. After a few awkward steps, Leena figured out how to maneuver on the slippery surface. It wasn't pretty, but at least it was progress.

After travelling a few feet, Leena paused and raised her left arm. She pressed a release catch on her wrist. A cover slid aside to reveal a small control panel. Leena tapped a few buttons before speaking again.

"Interface, activate infrared scanning."

An outline that resembled mapping schematics popped into view. Everything appeared identical. Blue lines covered milky white terrain. For as far as she could see, nothing stood out as unique. Leena steeled herself to give the report, desperately hoping to keep her emotions from showing through. Before she could speak, she saw something that made her gasp. A single feature, nothing more than a speck, glowed briefly orange. The spot faded quickly toward yellow, but Leena had already fixated on that single detail. Her eyes remained centered on that location as she stumbled in choppy, lumbering movements. Her heart thundered, the sound obscuring the icy, windblown shrapnel.

Several hard fought minutes later, she neared the source of her excitement. Her breath caught in her throat. On this new world, snow was a novel experience, but Leena recognized blood when she saw it.

"Andera!" she shouted, hoping in vain for an answer.

The word muffled inside her helmet. With the wind, the sound wouldn't travel far anyway. Leena stepped forward a few inches, intent on excavating the entire region barehanded if necessary. The front of her skid hit something and she pitched toward the ground. Leena thought she'd struck a rock or tree root until her hand came down on cold, yielding cloth. The material covered something warmer, though not by much.

Andera's shoulder.

The intensity of the resulting adrenaline surge

made Leena feel like insects had crawled under her scalp. She dropped carefully to her knees, attempting to avoid landing upon Andera. The skids on her boots and the emergency pack's weight made the task more difficult. Leena allowed the green canvas to glide off her shoulders and into the snow. With it out of the way, she tore into the powder with gloved hands.

Andera lay on her side, close to the surface. A layer of fresh, blowing snow had covered her. Combined with her falling body temperature, she had failed to register on the scanner. Leena kept a sharp eye on the readouts as she worked. Andera's heart continued to beat, but the graph on Leena's H.U.D. indicated an injury or infection. Coupled with the falling core temperature, Leena feared that hypothermia and shock were very real threats.

Leena scraped the snow away from Andera's body as quickly as possible. The roiling whiteout hampered her efforts, but she managed to dig Andera out. Once she'd completely revealed the unconscious form, Leena dove for the pack. She removed a silvery, rectangular cloth that fit within the palm of her hand. Leena grasped a corner and shook out a microfiber blanket. The flexible coils woven throughout activated with the motion.

Heat caressed Leena's face, but she hadn't time to savor the sensation. She tossed the blanket over Andera, tucking the coverlet around and underneath. Finally, she rolled Andera into her arms. Andera still wore a surveyor's helmet, for which Leena was deeply grateful. Although constructed for planetary study, the headgear should still provide some protection. Fueled by that assumption, Leena's eyes widened in horror when she spied the blue tinge of Andera's throat. Leena wanted to rip the helmet away to see Andera's face, but couldn't risk further exposure by removing it.

Leena suddenly remembered the intelli-computer scan indicating a possible injury. Time was of the essence. She cursed herself for not reporting in as soon as she found Andera.

"Leena Kyle to Captain Chase. I've found her. Send a flyer ship to my coordinates."

Only static responded. Leena tried twice more with similar results. Finally, she concluded that the surface conditions interfered with her transmission. Leena felt panic swirl in her gut. She had no idea what to do next. Raised in the city domes of the Alliance, Leena only obeyed orders. The Alliance told her what to do and when to do it. The Law of Legacy outlined her behavior as a citizen and her job as a Peacekeeper allowed her to fill a highly structured, strictly monitored role. She had no experience with self-motivated initiative.

Faced with what seemed an insurmountable dilemma, Leena felt frozen with indecision. Her arms tightened instinctively around Andera, holding the woman against her chest. She moved only when she felt Andera shiver. Leena glanced down at her, unable to see her features through the faceplate. Despite her inexperience with making independent decisions, Leena realized she had no choice. If she failed to act, Andera would die. She might die anyway, but it wouldn't be because Leena failed to act.

Decision made, the fog in Leena's mind dissipated. They needed shelter. A survival kit resided inside the pack, but Leena wouldn't be able to assemble it in this wind. She had to find a natural barrier that would allow her to put up the tent. Once she accomplished that, she could at least warm Andera up. Unfortunately, she couldn't carry Andera. Roughly the same height and weight, she recognized the impossibility.

Leena delved back into the pack and removed a retractable tumbrel. Normally, the gurney functioned by hovering above the ground. In this shifting, unpredictable landscape, Leena doubted that feature would work. It didn't matter. As she'd discovered, the slippery snow would provide all the assistance she needed.

She quickly constructed the sled and then shifted Andera onto the surface. Leena ensured the blanket wrapped tightly around Andera before moving to the front of the makeshift rickshaw. Leena retrieved the pack and then grasped the handles. She headed toward what appeared a particularly heavy strand of shriveled timber. Leena didn't know what summer was like on this world, but judging by the vegetation, she thought it probably as extreme as the winters.

Through sheer perseverance, Leena dragged the sled forward. The wind pushed and tugged as Leena stumbled in the heavy drifts. Within the space of a hundred yards, she had to dig the gurney out of the snow twice. By the time she approached the hoped-for refuge, Leena's muscles shook uncontrollably. Her breath came in panting blasts that sounded all the more intense inside her helmet. Leena searched desperately for any sign that she could stop, but other than the tiny trunks, didn't see anything to indicate a true windbreak.

A sob escaped her. Leena forced her legs to continue moving. Lift, step, lean forward, repeat...

She could barely lift her legs anymore. They felt leaden. Leena took another shuffling step and failed to pick her foot up far enough. She fell forward, her grip tightening upon the handles. Leena plunged face first toward the ground, managing to drag the sled halfway up her legs. Her helmet bounced off something hard even as Andera's weight pressed her lower body into the snow.

Leena took a moment to catch her breath, but didn't linger. Andera's condition was her primary concern, refusing to allow Leena the comfort of taking a rest. Instead, she released the handles and pushed up to her knees. Something, an obstacle buried beneath the snow, might just be the answer to her prayers. Leena had to investigate.

She slid her hands across the hard surface, dusting away inches of blowing, fallen powder. Leena discovered a raised platform, constructed of a stone-like substance she'd never seen before. Strangely smooth and rectangular, Leena found pitting in the rocky surface. By moving forward on her hands and knees, Leena excavated the top of the structure. It measured approximately two meters square. She located a metal ring near the far edge of the platform. The ring was the only unique feature she could discern.

Leena knew that another civilization had once lived upon this world. The scientists had discovered as much when they initially surveyed the planet as a possible haven from space travel. No one knew if the alien life forms still resided somewhere as yet uncharted. Leena considered the notion that she might find them hiding under her very feet. Disturbed and frightened by the prospect, one look at Andera made her decision. Leena took a deep breath and wrapped both hands around the pull. She heaved back and up, but the cover refused to budge. In the end, Leena utilized a cutting torch from her pack to remove the built up ice that prevented her from opening the lid.

A quick look down with the help of a wrist beacon assured Leena that they were alone. She let out a sigh of relief when she discovered steps leading downward. While she'd need to carry Andera from here, at least the end of the journey lay a short distance below. Lowering Andera into the subterranean space proved more difficult than Leena anticipated. Gravity worked both for and against her. Allowing Andera to plummet the short distance was out of the question. In the end, Leena held Andera against her chest, arms wrapped around her torso. Leena muscled them down the rough-cut stairs, one awkward step at a time. She leaned backward so as not to topple over.

Once finished with that chore, Leena wasted no time retrieving the pack. She disassembled the gurney and took it with her. She remembered the crusted ice she'd had to cut away from the cover and hesitated to close it behind them. Images of sealing herself inside a frozen tomb came to mind. Leena realized she hadn't a choice. She'd started to shiver. Even the Peacekeeper's uniform had its limits and they couldn't possibly make it back to her craft. In this whiteout, they couldn't *find* her craft.

It took only about twenty minutes for her to set up a crude camp at the bottom of the crypt. The small stove she retrieved from the pack provided light and heat. A silver cup of water heated on the burner as Leena focused on Andera.

They were inside some type of storage cellar. Nothing occupied this area and it was relatively free of snow and ice, though still extremely cold. Leena slid the pack under Andera's head. She had positioned her as closely to the stove as possible and steeled herself for what came next.

"There's nothing sexual about it. You're just checking her for injuries."

With that weak reassurance firmly in mind, Leena assessed the damage. She discovered a wide but shallow cut on Andera's forearm. It wasn't life threatening. The minor wound was the only open injury Leena found. She guessed it was the source of the blood she'd noticed on the scanner. Leena supposed Andera had simply succumbed to the extreme temperatures, not blood loss.

She injected Andera with a broad-spectrum antibiotic from the first aid kit and then bound the wound. Afterward, she rewrapped Andera in the blanket. She couldn't think of anything else to do. She concentrated on heating some emergency rations in the heated water. As the food cooked, Leena removed her helmet and gloves. She placed them aside and rested her head on her knees.

Leena felt exhausted. Her muscles trembled. Sleep beckoned and Leena relaxed for the first time in hours. She had almost dozed off when a voice startled her awake.

"Something smells good."

Leena scooted onto her knees beside Andera. She instinctively placed a hand on Andera's forehead. Searching for a fever just seemed second nature.

"Are you okay? How are you feeling? You scared the *hell* out of me!"

Andera smiled, the whiteness of her teeth in contrast to the dark bruises beneath her eyes. She attempted to sit and Leena helped her. Andera appeared pale and weak, but otherwise okay.

"I'm sorry about that. I was too far away from the survey team when the storm started. Needless to say, I couldn't even see the ship and communications wouldn't work."

"That's not surprising. I've had the same problem staying in touch with Chase."

Andera glanced around the makeshift campsite and frowned. She started to speak, but then shook her head. Finally, she focused on the stove.

"Do you have enough to share?"

Leena felt like an idiot. She retrieved the cup and carefully passed it to Andera, offering the mug handle first. She concentrated on tucking the blanket around Andera while she ate.

After a minute, Andera broke the silence. "Where are we?"

Leena shrugged. "Some kind of underground storage place? That's just an assumption since we don't know anything about the people who used to live on this planet. For all we know, this was their version of a penthouse suite."

Andera chuckled and passed the cup to Leena. Leena declined. Andera needed the nutrients more than she did. At least the stove had finally worked a little magic. Leena estimated the temperature had already risen ten degrees. It wasn't exactly balmy, but she'd take what she could get. Leena suddenly noticed that Andera's gaze rested briefly on her chest before flitting away. She finished the last of her rations in one large swallow. Andera passed the mug back to Leena and she glanced at Leena's torso once again.

The possibility that Andera might find her physical attributes appealing sent a thrill shooting through Leena's midsection. Leena had carefully kept her own romantic aspirations to herself for months. The continued glances made her want to blurt everything out in a rush. She almost did exactly that when she saw Andera look away toward Leena's discarded helmet and gloves.

"Is something wrong?"

"No, I suppose not."

"Come on," Leena cajoled. "I've never known you to withhold information."

Andera inhaled and puffed out her cheeks before releasing the breath in a rush. Leena thought the gesture endearing, regardless of it being one Andera performed when vexed.

"True enough, but only about scientific information."

"It's all right. There's no one here but us and I promise not to tell."

After another brief pause, Andera finally spoke up. "I thought you hated that uniform."

"Excuse me?" Whatever Leena had expected, this wasn't even close. That the remark was the most personal thing they'd ever discussed, threw her off even more.

"The Peacekeeper's uniform. When we found you on Earth's surface, you couldn't get out if it fast enough. You said it reminded you of unspeakable acts you committed for the Alliance."

Leena carefully considered her response. The past wasn't something of which she was particularly proud. Predominantly, she worried what Andera would think of her if Leena spoke her mind. Andera had her own experiences with Earth's law enforcers and they probably weren't very pleasant memories.

"There are so many layers to that response."

Leena fixed her gaze on a point between her booted feet, unable to speak while looking Andera in the eye. She couldn't bear to see the disappointment. "The only reason I ran from Bimark City dome was because I didn't have a choice. I stumbled across something in a computer file that painted a target on my back. They were coming for me."

"I know that already. You told the outpost leader that story when we found you."

Leena nodded. "What I didn't say was why I was in the computer to begin with. I'd been on a disbarment detail earlier that day. Afterward, I needed to enter the details into the census records."

"Disbarment," Andera snarled. "That's just a fancy way of saying you shoved a bunch of innocent people through the domes and exposed them to a death sentence. Earth is being blasted by solar radiation from a star about to go supernova."

"Don't you think I know that?" Leena fairly shouted the question. She had to take a moment before she could continue. "As a Peacekeeper, you're taught that only criminals are ejected through the dome. For a while, I even believed it."

"What changed your mind?"

Had Andera still sounded angry, Leena might not have answered. The quiet words gave her the courage to continue.

"The file I discovered. I learned the Cities Alliance routinely frames people so they can keep the population small. Apparently, resources aren't quite as unlimited as the leaders want us to believe. I felt sick. I wanted to expose them somehow, release the information to the people."

"But it was too late," Andera added. "They were

already on to you."

Leena nodded. "I had to run and I needed the uniform. I detested the suit because of what it stood for, but it was the only way to survive the surface conditions. It's the same reason I'm wearing it now. I couldn't have found you without it."

The gentle grasp of her hand finally encouraged Leena to look up. She didn't see disappointment, only compassion and understanding. Reassured, she squeezed Andera's hand.

"Everyone wants to believe their leaders have their best interests at heart. Don't blame yourself for that. Now, when are we getting out of here? As nice as this place is, I'm ready to get back to the station."

"Well, there's a problem with that. The blizzard's still going pretty strong. I'm afraid we're stuck until it blows itself out."

Andera seemed worried for the first time since regaining consciousness. "What about the rest of the search party?"

"There isn't any search party. I'm it."

"You can't be serious. Captain Chase sent you out to find me by yourself?"

"Uh, yes? I mean, I'm the only one who could have found you. My uniform was specially designed to withstand harsh environments. Anyone else could have died. I guess Chase must have realized..."

"You didn't have authorization, did you?"

Leena sputtered for a moment, seeking a way to deny the charge. Andera had seen right through her. "Fine. He said he couldn't risk losing more people in whiteout conditions."

"So you decided to come for me anyway? What were you thinking? Humankind hasn't seen this type of weather in centuries. We haven't any experience with it. You could have died."

The lecture took her completely off guard. Leena hadn't anticipated overwhelming gratitude for affecting a rescue, but this was too much. She'd gone against the new hierarchy to come after Andera. Anger caused Leena to throw caution aside.

"That's right, I did and I'd do it again without hesitation."

"Why?"

"Why? Because this expedition needs you. We have other scientists, but we don't stand a chance of survival out here without you. Chase was onboard pretty fast once he learned I'd left the base."

Andera lunged to her knees, moving well within Leena's personal space. She was close enough that Leena could see the gold flecks in her eyes. Andera seemed furious. "Don't hand me that. Anyone could take my place. That's just an excuse. What's the real reason you'd risk banishment for going against orders and coming after me all by yourself?"

"Because I love you, okay? Is that what you want to hear?" Belatedly, Leena realized what she'd said. She couldn't believe she'd just blurted it out like that. Leena rubbed a hand across her eyes. "You are so frustrating!"

Silence met her declaration. At first, Leena thought Andera was too shocked or annoyed to respond. Then Andera started to smile, taking Leena unaware once again.

"What?"

Andera shook her head. "It's about time, that's all. I've been waiting for you to say something since that first week back in Earth's caves. You really are stubborn."

"You knew?"

"Let's just say, I had an idea. You've faced down death squads single-handedly and braved Earth's surface without any resources whatsoever. Somehow, you survived to help a group of strangers escape to a new world. All this and you couldn't tell me you were interested? No, scratch that," Andera said with a raised hand. "I know you couldn't just blurt it out, but you might have shown me in some small way."

Leena went from angry to mortified in a flash. In many ways, Andera had a point. What Andera couldn't understand was that facing a troop of Peacekeepers intent on her demise wasn't anywhere near as frightening as admitting her innermost hopes and aspirations. Leena had simply killed the death squad. She didn't have to confide in them. She couldn't exactly do the same with Andera. Besides, Andera said she knew Leena had feelings, not that she reciprocated in any way.

"Why should I tell you anything?" Leena questioned gruffly. "You figured out how I feel, hell you even got me to admit it, but it doesn't mean anything."

"How can you say that? Of course it matters."

"No, it doesn't. It doesn't matter because you don't feel the same way. If you did, you'd have said so."

Andera's eyes widened, in what Leena assumed was shocked surprise. She looked like someone had slapped her. Suddenly, unexpectedly, her gaze softened. Andera reached out and gently cupped Leena's cheek. Leena flinched at the electrifying touch.

"You really don't know anything about women, do you?"

Leena almost pointed out that she knew about

women because she was one. The soft press of Andera's lips prevented her from speaking. All thoughts of argument ceased, words vanished from Leena's mind like wisps of smoke on the wind. Nothing existed save the taste of Andera's incredible kiss.

Andera took advantage of Leena's aroused moan to slip inside, past the barriers of lips and teeth. Tongues caressed. At the first stroke, Leena felt something in her heart shift. Carefully constructed barriers cracked, fissures spreading outward to release a lifetime of little hurts and cruelties. The sensation seemed as real as Andera in her arms. Past pain released in a torrent as love rushed in to swamp all. Within the blazing inferno of devotion and desire, the glacier of despair gave way, melting and flowing out of her soul.

Leena grasped Andera's shoulders, holding her almost desperately. Andera responded by pressing closer, pushing Leena backward. It came as a bit of surprise when Leena realized Andera lay atop her. The fire in Andera's eyes ratcheted Leena's arousal up another notch. Her skin felt ablaze, too hot for so many clothes. She had to get the suit off, craved the sensation of flesh on flesh.

"What are you doing?"

Leena barely registered the amusement in the words whispered against her lips. Seconds later, she understood. She had somehow, without knowing, opened the front of her uniform.

"I thought..." Leena swallowed and took a breath. "I don't know what I thought. It's too cold in here to take this any further."

"That and I was unconscious less than an hour ago. Still, it's a good thought. Why don't we put it into action when we get back to base?"

"I like the way you think. In the meantime, maybe we could just kiss a little more. We have to do something until the storm ends."

Andera's laugh caused Leena's heart to skip. Then those sweet lips parted and Andera moved toward her again. A sharp, short whine of static erupted from Leena's wrist communicator. The squeal interrupted the moment. An instant later, the static crackled again, but this time Leena heard a male voice.

"Chase to Kyle. The blizzard is settling. We have a fix on your location. Status?"

Leena wanted to curse Captain Chase's bad timing. Couldn't he have waited a few minutes? Or a few hours? While tempted to pretend she hadn't heard the transmission, she couldn't ignore the sparkle in Andera's eyes.

"Look at it this way," Andera invited. "The sooner we arrive back at the base, the quicker you'll be out of that uniform."

Okay, there was that.

Leena tapped her communicator to respond. "I'm all right. I have Doctor Sol. We took refuge in an underground bunker of some kind."

"Understood. A flyer is en route to you now. ETA, two minutes. Be on the surface standing by for pick up. Oh, and Kyle, good work."

The transmission ended and the women stood. Leena felt colder without Andera lying atop her, but the promise of more to come later motivated her to move. While Andera retrieved the discarded helmets and gloves, Leena packed the rest of their supplies. Neither spoke, but Leena didn't need to break the silence. The heated gazes shared between them were enough.

Leena had followed a group of seemingly crazy outcasts off a dying planet out of desperation. If she hadn't been running for her life, she'd never have considered leaving Earth. It was always her home. Now, she realized, home was wherever she found Andera. She donned her protective gear and headed for the surface, Andera on her heels. Bitterly frigid air rushed into the void when she opened the hatch. Moments later, Leena stood on the surface. The planet seemed eerily quiet without the howling wind. Sunshine blazed without storm clouds and bright light winked off the pure white snow. The breathtaking view astonished Leena and she glanced at Andera.

Despite the harsh conditions, Leena felt more joy and hope than she'd ever before experienced. Most of that had to do with the woman beside her. Oh yeah. She could live here.

S.Y. Thompson joined the Marine Corps at the age of seventeen and spent ten years serving her country. After she returned to the States, she joined the San Diego Sheriff's Department until taking early retirement. Now she spends time writing and playing with her dog and three cats.

Bedtime For Kedru Kits

By Linda North

Based on the novel Deep Merge

Faster, Wana. Go faster," Kaesah and Toni's three-year-old daughter, Chytris, cried excitedly as she clung to Toni's back in a bouncing ride that had become a bedtime ritual for the child.

Kaesah smiled as she watched the two beings she loved the most frolic around the central living area.

Destiny had taken Kaesah across the Universe where she found her beloved mate six years ago on a distant blue and green planet called Urtye and which Toni called Earth.

Toni pranced out of the living area and into Chytris' room, where she deposited the giggling child onto a low child's bed.

"Time for little kedru kits to sleep." Toni tucked the covers around Chytris and kissed her cheek, then knelt on the floor by the low, cot like bed.

"I want my Boo," Chytris said, her bottom lip stuck out in a pout.

Kaesah grabbed the stuffed bebum from the bottom of the bed. "Here you go, kitten." She tucked the toy under the covers, Chytris hugging it tightly. Toni referred to the toy as a 'teddy bear' and said she had a similar bedtime companion when she was a child.

Softly, Kaesah smoothed back Chytris' dark brown curls from her forehead and kissed her cheek. The curly hair and the girl's height were inherited from Toni, while the dark brown eyes and dark skin were from Kaesah and typical of the NaQwin race.

Chytris looked up into Kaesah's eyes. "Wanu, tell me a story. Curly locks and the three bebums."

"Wana told you that one last night." Toni had taken many of the Urtyne bedtime stories she heard as a child and fit them to NaQwin culture and animals.

"Tell me a story."

Toni said, "What is it we say when we ask someone for something?"

"Please."

Kaesah slid down beside Toni. "I have a story my wana and wanu told me when I was your age. A story of how the stars and Myrs were made. Do you want to hear it?"

With a wide grin, Chytris nodded.

Kaesah begin the story she had heard many times as a child. "Before time and space, there existed only Creator and Void. With a yawn, Creator rubbed the sleep from her eyes, blinked and looked around her. All she saw was Void. Sadly, she sighed, tired of the same nothingness she had seen upon wakening infinite times before.

How she longed for a different view instead of Void. Was there not another voice to soothe her ears instead of her own? Creator was alone with only the silence and stillness of Void. She grew tired of counting her fingers and hearing her sad sighs.

"I grow weary of nothing to see, and the sound of my own voice." Creator stood and frowned. She put her hands on her hips. "Void, why do you not adorn yourself with jewels and fabrics of many colors, so I may behold beauty? Why do you not sing songs both fast and slow, so I may dance?"

Void ignored her, content to be nothing and do nothing.

"Hmmm. I guess I will please myself then. I will sing a song from my heart and weave a dance from my soul. Yet, I will be sad since my eyes will behold only Void, and my ears hearing only my voice."

With eyes closed tight, she opened her mouth and sang from her heart. Her song filled Void with the sound of loneliness and the wish to hear another voice. Then she sang of how her eyes hungered for color and light.

From her soul, the steps of a dance emerged to lead her about Void.

Her song spun a new tempo and the steps of her dance wove the tapestry of a new dream. She sang as loud as she could, and she danced as fast as she could. Her song filled Void with the words of her heart. Her body moved and swayed, twirled and whirled around and around freeing her soul. Louder and louder, she sang, and faster and faster, she danced until she grew hot. The faster she danced the hotter she grew until she became a whirlwind of fire.

Fiery drops of sweat rolled down her arms and to her fingertips where she flung them into Void. Her song flowed in hot breaths, becoming puffs of mist into the cold of Void. The mist of her breath cooled many of the fiery drops of her sweat into beads.

Finally, Creator sang her song to its last note. She danced her dance to its last step. With eyes closed and head down, she said sadly, "I have sung my best song and danced my best dance, but do I hear one word of praise from Void?"

A faint whisper floated from somewhere in Void and then another. Many whispers floated about in void and surrounded her.

"Void, why do you mock me with echoes of my songs?"

Then from all directions in Void came a multitude of whispers to surround her. Each voice grew louder and became many different songs. Some songs were slow, some fast, but all blended together in perfect harmony.

Creator opened her eyes wide and stood astonished at what she beheld. Fiery globes without number filled Void, each swirling around Creator in a great dance. Many danced in their own light, several formed circles and danced in a group, and some adorned themselves with beads that swirled around them as they danced. Colorful clouds of varied hues hung above Creator's head. All sang of their birth and their destiny.

Joy overflowed within Creator. No longer was she alone. There were many songs to and dances to share, and the beauty of new friends to see. She lifted her voice and sang the Song of Creation with her new friends. So overcome with joy was she, tears fell from her eyes.

One little teardrop slid down her cheek to rest on her lips. This little teardrop caught the Song of Creation within it and floated away to sing and dance with Creator's new friends. That little teardrop was the first Myr. That is why all Myrs carry within them the Song of Creation, which is a blessing only the Navigator and her Anchor can hear."

Kaesah stroked fingers through her sleeping daughter's curly locks, and smiled. She sensed her mate's contentment and turned to stroke her cheek. The touch conveyed Toni's sleepy state. "I know a Kedru who needs her sleep."

Toni smirked. "Will you scratch my back?"

"What is it you say on Urtye? Scratch me and I scratch you back?"

"Something like that." Toni stood and helped Kaesah to her feet. Toni whispered into Kaesah's ear. "Of course I have other parts that could do with a scratch."

Kaesah muffled her giggle so as to not wake their daughter. "Toni, you are incorrigible."

"Always, darling, always."

Linda North is an unabashed romantic who believes in happy endings. She likes writing science fiction, fantasy, and historical fiction. She places her characters in exotic settings in the Sahara Desert to the far reaches of the Milky Way.

To Love Again - Carnival Dreams

By B.L. Clark

Jade and Rachel were reading in an oversized lounge chair out by the pool when Brianna came out of the house carrying a small, hard-bound notebook.

"Mama?"

"What's up?" asked Jade as she closed her book and set it on the table next to her. She watched as Brianna crawled up and sat between the two women. "Whatcha got there, sweetie?"

"You said that you and Mommy made this list for us to do as a family." Brianna opened the book and showed Jade one of the pages.

Jade couldn't help but smile when she saw that Brianna was holding the 'Family Bucket List' that she and Amy created over their time together. She glanced over at Rachel who was also smiling. The couple had been together for a little over a year now. They bought a house together and settled into couple-hood amazingly well. Jade felt blessed with the relationship that Brianna and Rachel had forged.

"Did you find something on the list that you wanted to do?" Rachel asked. She saw a smile cross the little girls face.

"I saw that there was a carnival in town," stated

Brianna.

Jade smiled at Rachel remembering their night at the carnival and then her times there with Amy. She and Rachel had gone in order to prepare Jade for taking Brianna. This was their opportunity.

"Yes, it is in town this weekend. Would you like to go?" Jade asked.

"I think it is a great idea," said Rachel.

"And we're all going, right?"

"Of course, baby girl. Why would you think that we wouldn't?"

"Because you and Mommy created the list for us to do together. Rachel is now part of the family, and I want her to be there with us."

"Of course I'll be there." Rachel was always amazed at the level of care and understanding of this particular seven-year-old. She had had it the whole time that she'd known Brianna. Rachel kissed the side of Brianna's head. She knew that she couldn't love this little girl anymore if she were her own.

∿∿∿∿

Jade parked the car in the lot and took a deep breath and slowly let it out. She'd done this the previous year with Rachel. They'd faced some of the demons that haunted this place for her. This is where she and Rachel had shared their first kiss, but it was and would always be her and Amy's place. Now, she was bringing Brianna, their daughter, to the place that shared so many happy memories, and the haunting dark cloud that Amy wouldn't be here to share it with them.

"Do you need a minute?" asked Rachel, concern written on her face.

"Yeah, I think so." Jade gave Rachel a weak smile and then turned her eyes to the entrance of the fair.

"Amy, what are we doing at the carnival?" Jade asked as Amy pulled her toward the entrance.

"We are here to have fun. Come on, Jade? Seriously? Who doesn't love coming to the carnival? There are rides, popcorn, funnel cakes, mini donuts, and games."

"All right. I will give it a chance since it seems to mean so much to you," Jade laughed.

The couple made their way to the ticket booth. Amy paid for their bracelets, and they headed through the carnival arches.

"Now, you have to start with one specific ride every time." Amy was leading Jade by her hand toward the ride that was now directly in front of the. "This sets the tone for the entire experience."

A couple of tears escaped from Jade's eyes. She wiped them away quickly and gave Rachel a small nod, hoping to reassure her, but it was really to set her own resolve that she could do this.

"Mama? Are you okay?" Brianna asked from the back seat.

Jade could hear the concern in her daughter's voice. "Yeah, I'm great, baby girl."

The three exited the car, and Brianna took ahold of each woman's hand as they made their way toward the entrance. After receiving their bracelets and tickets for games, they entered the grounds.

"Whoa," said Brianna, looking around at all of the flashing lights. "You and Mommy came here every year?"

"Yes, we did. I had my first kiss with…" Jade stopped in the middle of her sentence realizing that she'd kissed both Amy and Rachel here for the first time. She blushed as she looked over at Rachel who had her eyebrows raised and a knowing smirk on her face. Jade felt her nerves calm. "Okay, well the first ride always, always, has to be the Tilt-A-Whirl."

"Is it a scary ride?" Brianna asked. "It sounds scary."

"It was one of Mommy's favorites." Jade smiled at her daughter, and as they walked up to the ride, they were told to pick a car. "You pick one, baby girl."

Brianna looked at all of the cars and then pointed at the one car that appeared to be moving more than the others. Jade laughed and the three of them made their way to the back of the ride and into the car.

"Seriously?" Rachel said playfully as they sat down in the car, and it started to move around the circular track faster. "Like mother, like daughter."

Jade and Brianna giggled as the car moved around its track. The attendant came around doing their safety check and made sure that the cars safety bar was locked. He then spun the car causing Brianna to giggle even more.

Having survived two consecutive rounds on the Tilt-A-Whirl, they walked and rode on a children friendly roller coaster, and Brianna rode on the swings.

"Whoa, that ride looks neat," Brianna said, pointing at the ride directly in front of them.

Jade saw Rachel turn pale and a slight shade of green. She glanced and saw that it was the Zipper. Rachel hadn't fared well after that ride when they were here before.

"No, no it is not," mumbled Rachel.

"It's a fun ride, sweetie," started Jade, putting a hand on her girlfriend's back. "You'll have to wait until you are a little older and taller to ride on it."

"Will you take me, Rachel?"

"Um...er..."

"Bri, I don't think Rachel will be the one taking you on this ride. I will though."

"Why won't Rachel go on it with us?" asked Brianna

"Rachel got sick on that ride," Jade said. She and Brianna giggled while Rachel turned a little darker shade of green.

"It's okay Rachel, you can watch Mama and I then." Brianna gave Rachel a genuine smile and then hugged her.

The trio had been there for a couple of hours, and they decided to get something to eat and rest. Brianna and Jade found a seat while Rachel went to get the food.

"Are you having fun?" asked Jade.

"Yeah," Brianna said, but the cheer didn't reaching her voice.

"What's wrong, Bri? Are you too warm? Do you not feel well? Tell me."

"I miss Mommy." Brianna said this so quietly that Jade almost didn't hear her.

"Sweetie," Jade started as she pulled her daughter onto her lap. "I still miss Mommy, too. There is nothing wrong with that."

"You do?"

"Yeah, I do. Not a day goes by that I don't think about her."

Jade glanced up and saw the questioning look on Rachel's face. She mouthed Amy's name, and the redhead nodded.

❧❧❧❧

Rachel bought the three of them mini donuts to share and each some water for their snack. She remembered a story Jade once told her about how much she and Amy looked forward to the donuts when they came to the carnival.

"Bri, did you know that your mommy loved to get mini donuts when she and your Mama came to the carnival?" asked Rachel.

"She did?"

"Yep," Jade replied, winking at Rachel. "The first time that Mommy and I came to the carnival she made sure that I ate them with her..."

"Jade, they are all kinds of sugary goodness," Amy said as she pulled her date towards the concession stand.

"I know they are, but really? Before we go on more rides?"

"It is a tradition. You need to accept this and understand that you are going to eat a lot of mini donuts."

"You are pretty confident of yourself there. This is only our first date." Jade couldn't help it as her heart raced at the fact that Amy was discussing their future. And it appeared to be a long future.

"Call it a hunch. Now, let's move it. These donuts aren't going to eat themselves."

The couple moved to the concession stand, and Amy ordered the donuts while Jade found them a place to sit. Amy joined her, and sitting closer than necessary, she toasted Jade's donut with her own.

"To many, many more carnivals and donuts."

"Mommy was silly," laughed Brianna.

"Yes, she was," Jade said as she felt Rachel's hand

on her back.

They ate the cinnamon and sugar coated goodness, Rachel and Brianna teased Jade that they were going to wipe their sticky fingers on her. Rachel was happy to see the two of them laughing. After eating and cleaning their hands, the three walked around the grounds looking at the games, Brianna was trying to decide what game she wanted to play. They walked by the game where Rachel had won the goldfish the year before. Then they went by a couple of ring toss games, a dart and balloon game, and even a water game where you were to use the water to propel your jockey and horse along the course to the finish line. Rachel watched as Brianna watched the people playing.

"Mama, Rachel, look," Brianna said, excitedly.

The couple looked up and saw that Brianna was pointing towards the Fun House. Rachel and Jade both smiled. That was where their romance started, or where they had at least subconsciously allowed the idea of the romance to start.

They entered the Fun House, and as they entered the "Hall of Mirrors", Brianna was running between the different mirrors and laughing. Jade loved seeing her daughter so happy. After playing with the various fun mirrors, they entered the "Room of a Thousand Images."

"Whoa," said Brianna.

"Pretty cool, huh?" Rachel asked, kneeling down next to Brianna.

"There are so many of us," Brianna whispered.

Jade stepped away from the other two. "So, what are we going to do after this?"

Brianna looked next to her where Jade had been standing and saw that she was no longer there. She then looked at all of the mirrors showing Jade's reflection and tried to identify which was Jade, and which were fake.

"Mama, you're silly."

"Oh, I am?" asked Jade as she came up behind Brianna and hugged her.

"Yes, you are," said Rachel. She leaned over and kissed her girlfriend.

Once they left the Fun House, Brianna saw the goldfish game where Rachel had won her Olaf. She ran ahead of the two women and was looking at the various bowl and fish.

"Can I get Olaf a friend?" she asked, when Jade and Rachel caught up to her.

"You'll have to talk to Rachel on that. She is the one that won you the first fish."

"Please Rachel?"

"Okay, which one do you want?"

Brianna pointed out the fish that she wanted to go with the one she had at home. Rachel tossed the first ball and made it in the bowl. Brianna squealed and jumped up and down. The man who had retrieved the bowl handed it to Rachel, who in turn handed it to Brianna.

"Mama, look," said Brianna, holding the bowl up for Jade to see.

"This is a great addition to our family," Jade said, smiling at her daughter. "What are you going to name it?"

"Um, Steve," Brianna said, proudly. "Hi Steve, welcome to the family."

"Bri, sweetie, why Steve?" asked Jade, confused by her daughter's choice in name. She could also hear Rachel giggling behind her.

"It looks like a Steve to me." Brianna looked up at her mother and smiled proudly.

"Okay then, hello, Steve."

"What's up, Steve?" Rachel said, no longer able to contain her laughter any longer.

The fish was another standard goldfish, but this one had black specks on it making it easier to tell the difference between the two. Jade knew they were going to need to get a bigger bowl, but it was worth it to see her daughter happy.

As they made their way to the exit, Jade spotted the photo booth. She knew that if Amy were there that she would want to get the three of them in it and get a picture to mark their first trip to the carnival as a family.

"Come here," Jade said, pulling Rachel with her and Rachel pulling Brianna. "Picture time."

Rachel and Brianna exchanged looks and both grinned. Rachel took the fishbowl and Steve from Brianna. Brianna then crawled up on Jade's lap, and then both made a funny face for the camera, then they both smiled. For the last picture, Brianna requested that Rachel join them since they were all now a family.

After they arrived home, Rachel and Brianna went to introduce Steve to Olaf while Jade pulled out the photo album that contained the picture from her first date with Amy. She opened it up and laid the two picture strips side by side. On the left was the filmstrip of her and Amy, on the right was the filmstrip of her, Brianna, and Rachel. Jade felt Rachel wrap her arms around her from behind and softly kiss her neck. Jade leaned into the embrace.

"You are just as beautiful today as you were back then," said Rachel.

"I think I look older."

"You may look a little older, but that doesn't diminish your beauty. Brianna really does look like a mix of you and Amy. You can really tell it in the early pictures of you two."

"She does, doesn't she?" Jade ran her fingers across the pictures again before closing the photo album. "Are Olaf and Steve getting along?"

"Yep, and Brianna was headed up to put her jammies on."

Jade turned in the embrace and wrapped her arms around Rachel's neck. "You mean I might get you all to myself?" Jade leaned forward and captured Rachel's lips in a steamy kiss before she could respond.

The couple put Brianna to bed and then curled up together on the couch. Jade went about daydreaming about how perfect the day was at the carnival after she faced her demons.

The End

BL Clark lives in Southern Wisconsin. In her free time you can find her working on various story ideas, or playing with some form of technology, be it her computer, phone, tablet, or any other piece of technology she can get her hands on.

Good Night, Ever After

By Tara Wentz

Joooooosh, c'mon we're going to be late!"
"Keep your shorts on, Sport, we've got plenty of time."

Kellen rolled her eyes for the umpteenth time, but smiled all the same. As she sat on the couch scratching behind Chigger's ears, she couldn't help but think of all the things that had changed in her life. A chance meeting a little over a year ago brought about some of the worst and yet best times. She'd lost a father, gained a girlfriend and was shocked to find out that the mother she was told had died when she was a child was actually very much alive. At first she was fearful of reconnecting with her mother—what if she found they didn't have a lot in common or what if she disappointed her in some way. Kellen didn't know if she could handle losing her mother a second time. Joshlyn quashed all those fears first by just being there and second by reminding her time and again that her mother had always been there regardless that Kellen knew. She wasn't likely to go running. Her mother and Josh got along great and Kellen smirked, thinking how lucky she felt.

"Here I am rushing about and ready to go and yet you sit there with a goofy grin on your face. What's that all about, hmm?"

Kellen glanced over to Josh and then stood. "Just ruminating, that's all." Kellen gave her a once over taking in the sexy, toned legs encased in light colored shorts. The shirt clinging loosely to small, yet perfect breasts. A chain hanging around her long slender neck and diamond studs adorning—.

"Yoohoo, hey, eyes right here."

Kellen jerked her eyes to meet bright green ones and grinned sheepishly. "Maybe we could just stay home?"

"No. No way," Josh said laughing. "You've been on me the last hour to hurry up, so we are going." She grabbed her sweater off the couch and headed towards the front door. Before she could open it, Kellen placed her hands around Josh's waist and pulled her back against her chest.

Kellen leaned forward and softly caressed the outer edge of Josh's ear with her lips. Slowly she kissed her way down that beautiful neck and nipped lightly, pulling a gasp from Josh. Kellen turned her around and pushed her back against the front door. She effortlessly guided Josh's lips to meet her own, tracing first the upper lip and then drawing the lower lip between her teeth. Kellen pushed her hands into Josh's hair and pulled her impossibly closer to deepen the kiss. A stirring heat built in Kellen's pelvis making thought almost impossible. She tore her lips from Josh's and took a ragged breath.

"Mmm, you have no idea what you do to me, Kellen."

"Oh, I think I do," Kellen whispered, "It's nothing less than what you do to me."

Josh shuddered and brought her hands up to rest

against Kellen's chest, lingering only briefly before pushing Kellen back just a bit.

"As great as that feels, love, we have got to go or we will most definitely be late."

Kellen rested her forehead against Josh's and sighed. "Fun-sucker."

Josh laughed, grabbed her hand and pulled her out the door.

❧❧❧❧

Joshlyn grabbed a drink and pulled a chair up closer to the group. They were, indeed, a little late for the annual barbeque. After finally getting out of the house they dropped by to pick up Kellen's Mom, Anne. A lot of things had changed in the last year, but this was definitely a welcomed change.

Glancing over to the ball court she watched Kellen and Emerson bounce the ball back and forth before starting a new game.

"So, Josh, what's on the tap for the rest of your weekend?" Ami asked.

Ami was her go to for photo submissions for some nature magazines she worked for plus she was a very good friend. She was there during the tough times.

Josh swallowed the bite and then wiped her mouth. "I sent some of those pictures off to Robin so I'm waiting to hear back from her. Hopefully that will get her through the first portion of the book and then we'll start working on the middle portion."

"Oh, those were some good prints you sent." Anne commented. "I wouldn't want to be in her shoes trying to pick which ones to use."

"They did turn out well, didn't they?" Josh

agreed. She placed a hand on Anne's arm. "By the way, thank you for helping me go through them. I really appreciated it."

Anne covered Josh's hand and squeezed lightly in return. "It was my pleasure. I had a great time and the dinner you fixed was amazing."

Josh smiled. She *really* liked Anne and was overjoyed when she requested that Josh call her Mom if she wanted. Since the relationship with her own Mother was non-existent, she relished the one she had with Anne.

"What do you think those two are up to," Ami asked, nodding her head towards the court.

"Who knows with them," Josh chuckled. "Last time it was over who was the better player."

"Yeah and we know how that one turned out," Ami replied, shaking her head.

"It wasn't all bad though because it was my chance to get to know Kellen better."

"What happened last time?" Anne inquired.

"Kellen ended up flat on her back and out cold." Josh watched Anne wince. "Yeah, tough stuff over there swore up and down she was fine. Would you have expected anything less though?"

Anne grinned. "No, I really wouldn't. She always was stubborn—glad to see some things never change."

"It doesn't help that Emerson loves to goad her along. He doesn't care if he's right or wrong as long as he can get a rise," Ami quipped.

Joshlyn laughed along with Anne and sat back in her chair. She picked at her food and glanced around the group. She was so happy to finally be free of the stress that weighed her down over the last few years. These people were her family now and she couldn't be happier.

Anne leaned close. "You still going through with your plans tonight?"

"Yep," Josh answered and nibbled her bottom lip. "I don't know why I'm so nervous though."

"Oh, honey, if she loves you as much as I think she does and as much as I do, I don't think you have a thing to worry about."

Tears flooded Josh's eyes. "I got so lucky with the two of you," she sniffed.

"We are the lucky ones, sweetie." Anne pulled her close and gave her a hug.

Josh regarded Ami over Anne's shoulder and saw her blink the shine of unshed tears from her eyes. She smiled tremulously but then jerked out of Anne's embrace as Ami gasped and jumped to her feet.

"Oh no, not again," Josh groaned. She hopped up and followed Ami to the growing circle of people on the basketball court.

❧ ❧ ❧ ❧

"I can't believe you two," Josh blew an exasperated breath out, trying to get her hair out of her face. She had one arm around Kellen's waist and the other unlocking the door.

"How many times do I have to tell you it wasn't my fault?" Kellen grumbled, taking a step forward.

"I know, honey. You two just can't help yourselves can you?"

Kellen grinned and shrugged. This time truly wasn't either of their faults. Emerson was dribbling towards her and turned to his left. As he did, Kellen followed his motion and they both tried to put on the brakes as a toddler had worked his way onto the court.

For fear of hurting the young boy, they both tried to veer the same direction and ended up tangling feet with one another. Kellen tried in vain to step over Emerson's fallen form and almost succeeded…almost. Instead, she ended up flailing her arms before falling to the asphalt on her hands and knees.

"C'mon, just a little farther." Josh helped Kellen sit on the couch and crouched down in front of her. "Damn, you did a number on your knees."

"Eh, they don't hurt that much," Kellen answered, taking a gander at the raw mess.

"Ahuh, well let me get some antiseptic and bandages. I'll be right back."

Kellen leaned back against the couch and peered over at her dog, Chigger. He was thoroughly unimpressed with their arrival home. He barely lift his head to spare a glance in their direction before dropping it back to the arm of the couch.

"You've got the life, Chigger buddy." She scratched his back and contemplated the rest of the night. Her knees would alter things a little but not enough to worry about. Closing her eyes, she concentrated on the sounds Joshlyn was making in the bathroom. Such domesticity really and if her knees weren't stinging so bad it might be comical, but damn those asphalt burns hurt. A little tender loving care from the woman she loved more than anything never hurt though. The thought made her smile.

"What's got you grinning?"

Kellen opened her eyes to Josh standing in front of her. "Thinking of you, my love, thinking of you."

"Sweet talker," Josh quipped, but smirked in return. She knelt down in front of Kellen and opened the bottle of antiseptic. "Okay, this might sting a little."

Kellen sucked air between gritted teeth as Josh dabbed the cold liquid against her abraded skin.

"Sorry."

"S'ok."

Josh finished with the antiseptic, placed some antibiotic ointment on the bandage and adhered it to the skin. She repeated the process for the other knee and then placed her hands on Kellen's thighs.

"Doing all right there?" Josh asked.

Kellen nodded, but stared straight into her bright green eyes. She brought a hand up, slid her fingers into soft hair and cupped her palm against Josh's face.

"You are so beautiful."

Josh leaned into the touch. "May you always think so, Kel."

"I don't really think that is something you have to worry about." Kellen slid her hand back further and pulled Josh closer to her. She leaned forward and placed a tentative kiss on her lips. Feeling Josh lean even closer, she deepened the kiss. A small fire took hold deep down in her abdomen and built the longer the kiss went on. She tipped her head and broke the kiss off with a gasp. Nibbling her way across Josh's jawline, she sucked in an earlobe and then released it, letting her teeth grate across it.

"Cheese and rice," Josh panted. "You never fail to leave me breathless."

Kellen chuckled. "Like I've said before, honey, it's no less than what you do to me."

"Mmm, well maybe we should move this to the bedroom, huh?"

"Sounds like a perfect idea to me. You okay with me taking a quick rinse off first?"

"How about we share the shower so we can both

get done quicker?"

Kellen laughed. "I don't know how much faster that will be, but you're on. Let's go." Kellen stood and offered Josh a hand up. She didn't let go as Josh flipped off lights and they headed into the bedroom.

❧❧❧❧

The shower was, in fact, not fast at all. They both got sidetracked with the task at hand. Literally. Forty-five minutes and little to no hot water later found Joshlyn blowing her hair dry. Kellen had already finished and was getting settled in bed. She wrapped the cord around the dryer and placed it under the sink. She brushed her teeth then hit the light switch off before heading back into the bedroom. Kellen had all the lights off, but the room was dimly illuminated by a single candle burning on the night stand.

Josh walked closer to the bed. "My, don't you look comfy."

Kellen was sprawled in the middle of the bed with just a sheet pulled to her waist. "Oh, I'm definitely comfortable. You going to join me or just stand there?"

"From where I'm at the view really is pretty spectacular." Even in the low light Josh could see the blush spread across Kellen's features. It was such an endearing sight. After what Kellen had done to her, twice no less, in the shower it was amazing that such simple words could pull that kind of reaction.

Kellen patted the bed. "C'mon, don't leave a girl hanging."

"We wouldn't want that now." Josh unknotted the towel and let it drop to the floor. She crawled on all fours to where Kellen lay and then moved to straddle her hips.

"Hi," she said to a grinning Kellen.

"Hello there yourself. Come here often?"

Joshlyn sputtered before breaking out into a full belly laugh. "That was terrible." She loved this fun side of Kellen that a lot of people never got to see.

"Maybe so, but it made you laugh."

"That it did." Josh just stared at her. In all her life she never thought she'd find this kind of love. A tremulous smile broke across her lips. The emotions she was feeling were almost overwhelming sometimes.

"What?" Kellen asked quietly.

Kellen's hands were grasping Josh's hips and her thumbs stroked back and forth making goosebumps rise on her skin.

"Nothing really, I'm just so thankful to have you in my life."

It was one of those rare moments where words were not necessary. They both knew the extent of Joshlyn's comment and let it stand.

"So," Kellen cleared her throat. "Want to show me how thankful?" she asked, waggling her eyebrows up and down.

Joshlyn brought her hands up and palmed each of Kellen's breasts. She rubbed in light circles and then grasped a nipple between her fingertips and squeezed.

"Oh!" Kellen gasped.

Josh leaned down and took a nipple between her lips and sucked while squeezing the other nipple again. Kellen's hips rose and Josh ground down against her. She traced a path up to Kellen's neck and caressed the skin between her neck and shoulder with her nose.

"You smell so damn good."

"Please," Kellen rasped.

With her lips against Kellen's neck, Josh could

feel her erratic heartbeat and knew she was more than ready. She slid a hand down Kellen's torso, across the small patch of curly hair and between warm, wet folds to the awaiting hardened nub.

"I see someone is a little excited. You are so wet."

"A little excited? You've got me tied up in knots here, babe."

Josh chuckled. Slowly she moved her fingers around and across Kellen's clit, taking up the same movements as Kellen's hips.

"Oh Josh, that feels so incredibly good."

Josh leaned in close to Kellen's ear and dropped the tone of her voice. "I love making you feel this way, Kellen."

"I'm so close," Kellen whimpered and bit her lower lip.

"I know, just let it go, honey."

"I hate for it to be over so—," Kellen stopped mid-sentence as Josh slid two fingers deep inside her and kept her thumb moving over her clit. Josh knew it wouldn't be long now. She kept a continuous pace until she felt Kellen start to tighten underneath her.

"That's it, baby, let it go. Let me hear you," Josh whispered in her ear.

"Oh, God, yes…oh, oh…please don't stop!"

"Mmm, I wouldn't dream of it, love."

Josh pulled her closer and felt the tension coil tighter in her body. Kellen's legs stiffened and her hips rose slightly off the bed. As Kellen's fist tightened around the bed sheet, Josh inserted one last finger to send her completely over the edge.

"Sweet mother of…Holy hell, woman. Are you trying to kill me?" Kellen uttered.

Josh chuckled and continued to hold her until

her breathing slowed and the trembling subsided.

"Wow. I don't know where that came from, but, well, just wow."

Josh leaned up on an elbow and used a finger to wipe away a drip of sweat ready to fall into Kellen's eyes. "I love you so much Kellen…so, so much."

Kellen reached up with a hand and stroked her thumb gently across Josh's chin. "I love you, too, honey."

Josh kissed that thumb and pursed her lips. "Kel, I was wondering…um, uh, well do you think—,"

"Joshlyn, would you marry me?"

"Kellen, would you marry me?" Joshlyn blurted at the same moment.

They both stared in surprise at each other and then burst out laughing.

"Son of a bitch," Kellen wheezed over laughter.

"What?" Josh asked, wiping tears out of her eyes.

"You stole my thunder!"

"Excuse me? How exactly did I steal your thunder?"

"I had planned all along on asking you tonight. I even discussed it with my Mom."

Now Josh really started laughing. "You discussed this with your Mom?"

"Yeah, why?"

"Honey, I think your Mom is the one getting the best laugh out of this. I discussed it with her, too."

Kellen's jaw dropped causing Josh to reach up and close it while laughing again.

"That little sneak."

Josh nodded, "Absolutely!"

Kellen rolled Josh into her arms and then pulled the sheet up to cover them. When Kellen's chest started to shake with laughter again, she raised her head and propped her chin on a closed fist.

"I can't believe she knew already," Kellen started. She reached up and pushed a couple tendrils of hair back behind Josh's ear before continuing. "I'm surprised she hasn't been calling to find out how things went and all."

Josh blushed. "Well, I kind of told her I'd call her tomorrow in case we were, uh, busy this evening."

Kellen gave Josh an affectionate glance and then kissed her.

"Joshlyn Davis, I would love nothing more than to marry you."

Josh gulped down a swell of emotion.

"You say the absolute sweetest things. I would love nothing more than to become Mrs. Kellen Reynolds."

The silly grins on their faces couldn't have been doused even if they tried. Kellen lifted the candle snuffer and extinguished that flame instead.

Josh snuggled closer to Kellen. "Goodnight, baby. I love you."

"I love you, too, honey. Goodnight."

~The End~

Tara lives in Missouri with her partner and has been in the medical field for over 25 years. When not working or writing, Tara likes to read, dabble with photography and watch sports. She has two novels, Traffic Stop and Deception by Design, and is currently at work on her third.

Arizona Honeymoon

By Sandy Dugger

The air hung stagnant and beat down on the old weathered porch. Bailey leaned against the railing and fanned herself with her new cowboy hat as she stared at the cloudless sky. She loved Shayla and would do anything for her, but she was starting to rethink their plans of visiting Arizona during the middle of the summer. Dust exploded into the air to her right. She ran her hand through her short curly hair before she placed the hat back on her head and watched the dust storm that was fast approaching. It didn't take long before a speeding car come into view. The car had barely come to a stop before a tall blond jumped from the car and hurried to up the steps. A quick hello was murmured as the woman rushed passed her and disappeared behind the slamming screen door.

The driver was slower to exit. Bailey skipped down the steps and strolled to the car.

"Can I help you with your bags?" Bailey asked. She knew they had people to help with their bags, someone had helped with her bags, but since she was there she would help the new arrival.

"That would be great," The woman said. With a push of a button the trunk popped open.

Bailey started to pull bags from the trunk and

almost dropped the bag in her hand when there was a loud scream. When she stood up and looked over the top of the car she found the driver caught by the woman she had just met named Jo. With two heavy bags in each hand she found her progress stopped by a dusty Hispanic woman.

"It's ok ma'am. I got these," The cowgirl said and wrapped her calloused hands around Bailey's and took the bags.

"Sally, come here and give me a hug," The driver said and pulled Sally into an embrace.

"Keri, it's great to see you again," Sally said and dropped the bags and embraced the woman.

Bailey shrugged and grabbed two bags Sally had dropped and made her way to the porch. She set them down and before she could go back for the rest Sally walked up with the remainder of the bags.

"Thank you for the help," Sally said.

"No problem." Bailey held out her hand, "Bailey."

"Sally," The cowgirl said and brushed her thumb over Bailey's knuckles. Bailey recognized the move and quickly retrieved her hand.

"So you work here?" Bailey asked and returned to her position against the pole.

"Yeah I've been working here going on eight years now." Sally removed her beat up hat as she pulled a handkerchief from her back pocket and wiped the sweat from her brow.

"How can you get used to this heat?" Bailey asked and removed her hat again to fan her face. The motion did nothing but move the hot air around her. The only relief was to cool the sweat that had beaded on her forehead and run down her face.

"I was born here, I'm used to it."

"I've only been here a few hours, with my wife, and I don't think I could ever get used to this heat. It's nothing like back home," Bailey said.

"Oh well it does take some getting used to. I had better get back to work." Before Bailey could say anything Sally turned and disappeared down the stairs. She flinched when she heard the screen door slam again.

The blond from early who rushed by again hurried past her and made her way to Jo and pulled the woman into her arms. "I've missed you guys so much."

"You too. You've gotten so big Rose," Jo said and pulled back from the woman and looked at the small bump on her stomach. She hesitated a moment before she put her hands on Rose's bulging belly.

"I know. Sorry I rushed by so fast earlier. I almost didn't make it to the bathroom." Rose covered Jo's hand and pulled it to her stomach.

"I asked you miles back if you wanted me to stop," Keri said and rubbed Rose's back.

"I know, and I should have had you stop. I guess I didn't realize how much weight two babies would be on my bladder," Rose said and leaned her head on Keri's shoulder.

The screen door slammed again and Bailey felt a hand on her back. She turned and smiled at her wife.

"Why don't you come inside? It's a lot cooler. Jo said our cabin should be ready in about an hour," Shayla said and placed a quick peck on Bailey's cheek.

"I was just admiring the view," Bailey said. "I don't know how much writing I'm going to get done here. It's so damn hot."

"That's fine. This is our honeymoon after all." Shayla said and turned Bailey to her to give her a real kiss. Bailey leaned into the kiss and pulled Shayla to her.

Seconds passed before Bailey pushed her away but still held her in her arms. "Why did you want to come here? And in the summer no less, it's only a couple degrees hotter then hades," Bailey said and brushed at the sweat that started to drip down Shayla's cheek.

"It's cooler if you come inside," Shayla said and pulled away. A few steps from the door she stopped and held out her hand. Bailey took the hand that was offered her and followed her wife inside. The cool air chilled the sweat that had peppered her body. She shivered and Shayla squeezed her hand.

"I don't know why you were standing out there," Shayla said and continued to pull her through the house.

"I wanted to get a feel for the place. I was thinking of maybe writing a book about the Arizona summer. I have to be able to experience it if I want to do a good job describing it," Bailey said and sat at one of the tables in the dining room.

"I'll get us some lemonade," Shayla made her way to the buffet and retrieved two tall glasses.

"Drink. You need to stay hydrated. It's not like back home," Shayla said when she placed the two glasses on the table.

"So what are you looking forward to doing now that you've seen the place?" Bailey asked Shayla.

"I don't know. I know the over-night is out but I was looking forward to doing a few rides, but I'm ok with spending just as much time by the pool," Shayla said and ran her slim fingers over the moisture that gathered on the glass.

"I know I want to do some writing, but I'm looking forward to learning about the horses. You know I was thinking about writing that western." Bailey took another sip from her glass.

"I remember, and I can't wait to read it," Shayla said and reached across the table and took Bailey's hand in hers.

The group from outside wandered into the living room with another older cowgirl in tow.

They stopped when they reached the table.

"Thank you for helping with our bags earlier. My name is Keri and this is my wife Rose." The driver from earlier said and held out her hand.

Bailey stood and shook Keri's hands then Rose's. "You're welcome. Glad I could help. And this is my wife Shayla. Would you like to join us?"

"Oh no thank you, we're going to pop into the kitchen, but if you're free at dinner would you like to join us tonight?" Keri asked as the other three women continued through the swinging doors.

Bailey looked to Shayla and the slight nod was all that she needed. "We would love to join you for dinner. Seven ok?"

"Perfect. We'll see you then," Keri said and excused herself to follow the group of women who had just exited the room.

"I hope that was ok?" Bailey said.

"That's fine. We'll be here a week and it will be nice to meet new people," Shayla said and leaned over and gave Bailey another kiss.

"Excuse me," Jo said beside the swinging doors. "Your room is ready."

"Perfect timing," Bailey said and started to giggle and pulled away from Shayla to get the key from Jo.

"Your bags have already been delivered, and here is your room key. It's cabin ten. Just down the trail and on the left. It's the second to last cabin," Jo said and handed Bailey the key. "Just a suggestion during the day it is a good idea to keep the windows cracked and the door open with the fan running to get a cross wind. We have never had a theft here and if you keep the fan going the wind will help a bit with keeping the room a little cool. But if you do chose to spend the day in the room you can turn on the air conditioning and close up the room. I would suggest turning the air on an hour before bed."

"Thank you. Uh, actually I'm a writer, and I will be spending most of my time indoors, do you think it would be better to write in the room or can I come up here to write?" Bailey asked when she retrieved the key.

"You can come up here. If you sit at that window you will have a great view of the barn and the mountains," Jo said and pointed to a table with two chairs.

"Thank you," Bailey said before she returned to her wife.

"I want to go to the room and freshen up for a bit. Do you want to come with me?" Bailey asked and grabbed Shayla's hand.

Shayla leaned in and whispered, "Or we could go back to the room and get sweaty and make a reason to freshen up." Shayla kissed Bailey's neck.

Bailey shivered and grasped Shayla's hand harder.

Shayla leaned in and kissed Bailey. A minute later Bailey pulled away and without another word pulled Shayla to the exit. Silently she pulled her wife behind her as she followed the trail. The mountains loomed in the distance were unlike any Bailey had seen, but she didn't have time to stop and gaze at their beauty. The only thing she had eyes for was cabin number ten that was just ahead.

Without a word she slid the key into the lock and opened the door. The room was stifling but she didn't care, the only thing on her mind was the hand that squeezed hers. The bed was to the left and even though she had been with Shayla for four years and made love more times then she could count she knew this time was special. It would be the first time since they had said their vows. Something she had never dreamed that would have happened. They lived in Oregon, and it had been legal for a few years, but they had both agreed that they would not want to get married until it was legal in every state. And now a familiar thumb was playing with the silver band inlayed with diamonds.

"I love you." Three simple words, but words Bailey knew she would never grow tired of hearing coming from her best friend, her partner, her wife's lips. She turned to Shayla and took both her hands in her own.

"I love you too. More than life itself." Bailey pulled Shayla to her and wrapped her arms around her body and whispered in her ear, "I can't believe you're my wife. This is a day I never thought would come."

"I feel the same." Shayla's breath on Bailey's neck sent shivers down her body. "Make love to me."

Bailey stood back and slowly started to unbutton Shayla's shirt. With each button creamy flesh appeared. When the last button was released she slowly slid her hands up Shayla's center and brushed her fingers across her shoulders till the shirt fluttered to the floor. Sweat started to pepper Shayla's skin and Bailey reached around and released Shayla's bra, it quickly joined the shirt on the hardwood floor. Another moment passed before Bailey reached down and released the button holding Shayla's slacks. Shayla stood bare before Bailey and before she could reach out, Bailey hurried and whipped her tee-shirt from her head and scrambled out of the rest of her clothes.

Heat surrounded Bailey's body like a warm blanket. She looked at the comforter and slowly walked to the head of the bed and tossed back the blankets and lay down on the crisp cool sheets. She held out her hand and her wife crawled to her, her thick braid lay heavy on her back as she crawled on top of Bailey. The braid fell to the side when she leaned down to capture Bailey's lips with her own. Bailey moaned into the kiss and wrapped her arms around Shayla to pull her body to her own, till not even air could pass between them. Shayla's weight settled on her and she moaned into the kiss. Blunt nails raked across Shayla's damp back. Shayla moaned into the kiss and Bailey rolled her over and forced her knee between Shayla's open legs.

Bailey leaned back and gazed into chocolate eyes that she had fallen in love with over fifteen years earlier. Shayla closed her eyes and Bailey leaned down, when only a breath separated their lips she whispered, "I love you."

Once the words were uttered Shayla lunged up and took Bailey's lips with her own. The kiss was fierce and Bailey felt the desire in Shayla's lips, and the heat coming from her center as it seared her leg. She leaned into, and drank in the moan Shayla gave. She had wanted to take her time, but she knew she had forever to take her time, now all she wanted was to take her wife over the edge. Again she rolled over and pulled Shayla on top of her. Shayla gave a squeal when she found herself on top of her wife. Bailey grabbed Shayla's pert ass and pulled her up her stomach.

Shayla gave Bailey another searing kiss before she pulled back and sat up. On her knees she slowly inched up Bailey's body. Bailey pulled her arms close and threaded them through Shayla's spread legs until she held her ass in the palm of her hands and pulled her body to her mouth. Bailey couldn't wait for Shayla to lower herself and reached up and dragged her tongue through her wife's center. When her tongue circled Shayla's clit music met her ears when Shayla let out a moan. Shayla's legs shook before she settled on Bailey's skilled tongue. Bailey kneaded Shayla's ass and moaned into her core as Shayla's juices coated her tongue. She forced her tongue as far into her as it could, and hummed as she was rewarded with a moan from her wife. Shayla started to grind against Bailey's mouth. Seconds passed before Shayla leaned forward and grabbed the headboard. With her pert breasts swaying so close Bailey struggled to free her left hand. When her hand was freed she reached up and pinched and twisted Shayla's right breast. The minutes ticked by as Shayla continued to ride Bailey's face like a wild horse.

Unable to deal with the pressure forming between her own legs Bailey reached down and ran her fingers through her own damp curls. The moment her finger met the bundle of nerves she moaned into Shayla's center and the woman above her began to grind harder. The minutes ticked by as both women continued to edge closer to their orgasm. Bailey pulled her hand away from Shayla's breasts and slowly entered her with two fingers. Two pumps of her fingers was all it took before Shayla captured Bailey's head with her powerful thighs as she tumbled over the edge. The moans that came from Shayla pushed Bailey over moments later.

As Shayla came down from her orgasm she scrambled off Bailey and kneeled between her legs. Bailey still had her fingers between her legs and Shayla brushed them away and leaned down and flicked Bailey's sensitive clit with the tip of her tongue. Bailey's body jerked at the touch. Shayla slid two fingers inside Bailey and moaned as Bailey ground against the invading digits trying to pull more of them into her. Bailey's chest heaved with every stroke against her velvety walls.

Shayla again flicked her clit before she rose up and captured a pert nipple between her lips. Bailey reached up and grabbed Shayla's braid and pulled her to her chest. She couldn't stop the moan that passed her lips with Shayla captured her nipple between her teeth and pulled. Bailey started to pant with every thrust of the invading fingers and when Shayla brushed her clit with her thumb she couldn't stop the scream that escaped when she fell over the edge. Shayla continued to pump into her and flick her clit keeping her orgasm going until Bailey grasped her hand as the feeling became too intense.

Shayla fell onto Bailey, and when she pulled her fingers from inside her, Bailey felt empty. The room was boiling and sweat coated their bodies. The fan helped cool the sweat that peppered their skin. With Shayla laying against her Bailey ran her fingers along Shayla's sweaty back enjoying the feeling of her wife as she shivered at her touch.

"I love you," Bailey said before she kissed the crown of Shayla's head.

Shayla looked up and gazed into Bailey's eyes before uttering the same words. She turned her head and snapped it back to Bailey. "Shit we have to get up. We have thirty minutes to meet the group back at the house for dinner."

Bailey bucked her hips and Shayla slid off. "We need a shower."

Twenty minutes later the two women were dressed and hurrying up the trail to the main house.

They entered the dining room and Rose and Keri looked at them skeptically. Before they even made it to the table they had been waved off to get their plate for dinner. They hurried over to the buffet and made their way to the table with their plates loaded with meat, potatoes and vegetables. Bailey set her meal down and made her way back to the buffet to grab two tall glasses of lemonade. She returned to the table and jumped right into the conversation.

"So I don't know if Shayla already asked, but what do you two do?" Bailey asked Rose and Keri as she cut off a large chunk of meatloaf. The food hit her tongue and she hummed as she savored all the flavors.

Rose smiled at Bailey before she spoke. "Watch what you eat here, the food is great and you would think with all the work you do here you would lose some weight, but I always seem to leave here heavier."

Keri reached over and placed a hand on Rose's stomach. "This time is totally different, but to answer your question I'm a doctor and Rose runs the bed and breakfast we own."

"Wow. Where's your bed and breakfast?" Shayla asked before she took a bite of her mashed potatoes.

"Upstate New York. So what do you two ladies do?" Rose asked and sipped from a glass that was covered with moisture. When she set the glass back down she trailed her fingers through the water that covered the glass.

"Well, I own a bookstore and Bailey is a computer programmer by day and an author by night," Shayla said and smiled at Bailey before giving her a peck.

"Oh, what type of books do you write?" Jo asked as she paused on her way to the kitchen with an armload of dirty dishes.

Bailey felt the blush rise in her cheeks. She would have replied but she had just stuffed another fork full of meat into her mouth, but she didn't need to as Shayla spoke up.

"She writes lesbian romance stories."

"Oh, that's cool. How many books have you written?" Keri asked.

"She has nine already published and another will be released next month," Shayla said and took a drink from her glass, and when the ice hit the bottom of the glass she stood and reached for Bailey's almost empty glass. "Can I get anybody a refill?"

When she made her way to the table she had four sweating glasses grasped in her hands.

"So Bailey what are you writing now?" Rose asked as her hands rubbed her bulging belly.

"Actually I haven't even started anything. Life has been a bit hectic recently. I've been helping my sister with her daughter while she goes back to school to get her masters, and then I have a full time job. Now that were finally done with the wedding maybe I'll have a little time to actually sit down and write," Bailey said and pushed her empty plate away. She wiped her lips and laid the cloth napkin on the plate.

"You should tell them your story," Jo said to

Keri as she reached across Bailey and picked up her discarded plate.

"Really? This sounds interesting," Bailey said and rubbed her hands together.

Keri turned to Rose and raised an eyebrow. "Well, it is an interesting story?"

Shayla set the four glasses on the table and handed them to the ladies, "We all have interesting stories." She bumped shoulders with Bailey, "Even we have an interesting story, but I hope she doesn't write about it. I want it to just be ours."

"I promised you I wouldn't," Bailey said and stretched her neck to give Shayla a kiss and then turned back to her dinning companions. "Plus I hope to be with her forever and I'm sure there are bound to be some things that will happen that will end up in print."

"I guess everybody has some story to tell. But we went through a lot to get here," Keri said and grabbed Rose's hand. "I don't know if Rose would want our story written either."

Rose turned to Keri and pulled her knuckles to her lips. She peppered each knuckle with a kiss before she spoke, "Baby the road we took to get here was long and bumpy, but I would walk it again just to spend one day with you. I don't mind telling Bailey our story, but your part is the one that could be rough to tell, and I don't think I could tell it or hear it with all these hormones rushing through my body. If you want to tell them that's fine with me."

Keri smiled at Rose before she turned to Bailey. "What Rose said is true, our road to here was rocky, and I'm sure you are a great writer and I don't mind telling you it, but I think tonight isn't the best time. We had a really long day and I think I need to get my wife and two kids into bed."

"Two? You're having twins?" Shayla asked and her eyes lit up.

Bailey also smiled at the couple. She couldn't wait for the day when she could have kids of her own with her wife, but for now Shayla and her would have to make due with helping her sister raise her daughter. Angel was about to start junior high school and they had been blessed that Morgan was doing well with her remission. They had all decided it was best to wait till after the wedding to start working on adding anybody to their family.

"Yeah, I found out when Keri and I were getting to know each other that twins run in my family," Rose said and continued to rub her stomach.

"But that's a part of the story that we'll tell you later. I really need to get Rose to bed, she doesn't tend to stay down too long with two little ones using her bladder as a punching bag," Keri said and stood. She held out her hand and Rose took it and gingerly got to her feet.

"I can't wait to hear your story," Shayla said and reached for Bailey's hand that rested on the table. She gave it a gentle squeeze.

"I can't wait either," Bailey said.

"Well then we should get together tomorrow so we can talk," Keri said and wrapped her arm around Rose before she pulled her close.

"That sounds perfect. I think we should be heading back to our room too," Bailey said.

Bailey reached for Shayla's hand and followed Keri and Rose out of the main house and down the path to their cabin. The two groups didn't say anything as the night animals serenaded them as they made their way back to the rooms.

Rose and Keri continued down the trail when Bailey and Shayla stopped at the deck in front of their cottage. Without saying a word they both sat in one of the rockers, their hands never broke contact as they started to rock and listen to the music of the night.

Bailey allowed her head to fall to the left and watched as her wife continued to move back and forth with the motion of the chair. Her eyes misted the longer she continued to stare. They had been married for only a day, but the woman next to her had been her whole life from as long as she could remember. She squeezed the hand that was still wrapped in hers.

Shayla stopped the rocker and the right side of her lips raised into a smile that turned Bailey's insides into jelly. She was glad she was already seated or she would have dropped to one knee.

"Are you ready for bed?" Shayla asked.

"I'm not tired, but I would like to lay in bed and hold you," Bailey said and reached down to kiss Shayla's knuckles.

"I would love that too." Shayla stood and pulled Bailey to her feet. The bookstore owner pulled Bailey close to her and kissed her. It wasn't a kiss that curled Bailey's toes or made her go weak in the knees, but it was a kiss that Bailey knew she would long to feel for the rest of her life. Silently they walked into the warm cabin and closed the door.

Life was full of stories, and as the Arizona animals made sweet music for the two women behind the closed door they continued to add words to the pages of their life.

Sandy Dugger lives in Arizona and spends her days

asking users to reboot their computers and her nights sitting at her computer writing her next novel. From a young age she has always wanted to entertain people. She hopes to continue entertaining her readers for years to come.

The Dental Hygienist's Dilemma

By Alison Solomon

Give me a sign Siri! Tell me where I'm meant to be, because I don't believe this dreary dental clinic is it."

I don't usually talk to my cell phone, but today I'm desperate. This morning I had no fewer than three patients who all told me they know the importance of flossing, but couldn't explain why they never do it. It's lunchtime and I'm frustrated and out of sorts. I take a large bite out of my alfalfa and quinoa whole-grain sandwich and bring up my Facebook app.

'Gulfport Library dedicates Florida's first and only LGBT collection.' I stare at the Facebook headline and know one hundred percent that Siri is personally sending me this message. A public library that specializes in LGBT books? It's the answer to a bookworm's prayers. For the rest of the afternoon I imagine myself sitting in a sun-filled library, helping earnest lesbians find their favorite author's latest novel, instead of spraying debris-filled mouths with water, and scraping and polishing dirty teeth in this grey Philly suburb.

"But you're not a librarian and you live a thousand miles away," my best friend Carmen remonstrates when I tell her my new plan—to get a job in the Gulfport library.

"I could be a library assistant. Keeping people's mouths clean can't be that different from keeping bookshelves clean and tidy."

"You would seriously move to Florida, land of hanging chads, rat-infested palm trees, and unbearable heat?" Carmen looks as horrified as if I'd just ordered a plate of spare ribs instead of my usual veggie stir-fry as we sit down to our weekly dinner together.

"The latest census shows one-third of the Gulfport population there identifies as LGBT. Imagine how much that increases my chances of finding The One." If Carmen is tired of my preoccupation with The One, she never says so. Maybe because she knows it's been two years since I had a steady girlfriend and even longer since I was in a relationship I thought might be forever.

"Yeah, but all those lesbians are probably over sixty five, tottering around on walkers. Whoever heard of a thirty three year old relocating to Florida? It's where you go to retire and die, not to meet hot bitches. If you want to be surrounded by cool dykes, go to West Hollywood, or Portland, or even Northampton."

The thing is, I'm not sure if I do want to meet cool dykes. Two months ago, at Carmen's suggestion, I signed up for OKCupid. At first, I couldn't believe all the women who were on the site—and once I got to know them, I couldn't believe *any* of the women on the site. Kim said she was a feminist and then came to our first date wearing a ripped tank top that had the logo, "Don't pretend to read my T-shirt, Just enjoy my Tits." Michelle said she was 100 percent lesbian, then admitted that the week before, she'd screwed a guy "'cos I was bored, ya know?" Beth suggested we get a drink and seven shots later confessed, "When I saw your profile online, my first thought was that no-one could be that boring. So I had to check you out." Was it the part about Longwood Gardens being my favorite hangout? Or that the cutest female I could name was my cat? At that point, I picked up my purse, collected what little dignity I had left, and deleted my online profile.

"Join the softball league," Carmen's latest conquest tells me the next time we're drinking salted caramel frappuccinos at our local coffee shop. "It's the next best thing to a weekly orgy."

"I don't have a sporting bone in my body." I wipe away the frothy mustache I can feel on my upper lip. "And anyway, don't believe everything you hear. I dated a softball player once, but when her team got together, all they did was bitch about the umpires, relive every run they scored and agonize over every play they missed. I couldn't get out of there fast enough."

When I get up to go to the bathroom, I overhear Carmen apologize for my negativity. "She used to be such fun," she whispers, "but lately, she's just kinda stuck."

It's true. I am as stuck as an old sandal held together with gorilla glue. That's why I figure a move to sunny Gulfport, may be just the answer.

❧❧❧❧

"But how will you get the library to hire you? Don't you have to be qualified or have a certificate or something?" It's three weeks after I first dropped the bombshell about my impending move, and Carmen is looking worried. For the first time she's beginning to think I may be serious.

"I'll astound them with my literary knowledge." I say. "I'll tell them how I've kept a record of every novel I've read since ninth grade in my book journal. And if all else fails, I'll offer to screw the head librarian." I spear a piece of dark green asparagus and pop it into my mouth.

"Who even uses libraries these days? Everyone just downloads books onto their e-readers. The only people who go to libraries are the homeless."

"How would you know, if you never go to one? If Gulfport has an LGBT collection, then obviously all the lesbians must frequent the library."

Carmen sighs. "You're doing a geographical."

"A…?"

"It's what we call it in AA when someone thinks that by moving, they'll turn their life around. It doesn't work, because wherever we go, we take all our emotional baggage with us. You have to sort out your life here, not just believe that a change of scenery is the solution to all your problems."

She has a point, but I happen to know that this time, she's wrong. I am heading to Gulfport with a plan: meet a never-ending stream of lesbian book lovers, find one who is serious-minded, political and not bad-looking, and live happily ever after. Simple.

❧ ❧ ❧ ❧

It takes a lot longer to pack my Kia Soul than I thought it would. My intention was to sell everything and leave unencumbered, but even after giving away the items I couldn't sell on Craigslist, I still can't squeeze the remaining boxes into the trunk and backseat of the car.

"You couldn't fly, like everyone else does, and have your stuff sent?"

"You know how much I hate airplanes. Anyway, I think the drive will do me good. Clean out the cobwebs."

"What the heck is in here?" Carmen asks as her knees buckle under the weight of a small box she tries to move to accommodate a bag filled with sheets and towels.

"My radical feminist book collection. I—"

"Dump it! You said you're only taking essential stuff you absolutely can't do without." She pulls the tape off the top and peers inside. "You need your linens a whole lot more."

"Not true," I argue, "I can go to any store and buy new bedding, but where am I gonna find classics like Cherrie Moraga and Kate Millet?"

"Hello? How about in the Gulfport LGBT library collection?" Touché.

Grudgingly, I let go of Mary Daly's *Gyn/Ecology* and Dorothy Allison's *Skin*, but I draw the line at Andrea Dworkin's *Our Blood*.

When the car is finally filled to capacity except for one small corner in the back, I bring out Ms. Kitty who is smiling contentedly in her carrier, having been dosed with more catnip than she's seen in her entire young life.

"Promise you'll come back if it doesn't work out?" Carmen gives me a fierce hug and I feel myself choke up.

I smile and wave at her as I pull away, but inside my stomach is starting to churn. What if she's right? What if I'm making the biggest mistake of my life?

My first stop is The Molly Pitcher Service area on the New Jersey Turnpike. I get gas, treat myself to a Starbucks, then pull into the picnic area. Ms. Kitty gives a little mew, which is perfect timing as I was planning on taking her onto the grass anyway.

An older man is walking a mean-looking bulldog, so I carry Ms. K. in the other direction across the grass toward the picnic tables where a woman in a black leather jacket is reading from a kindle, a small dog beside her. As we approach, the silky spaniel-mix looks up and sniffs eagerly.

"Maxi loves cats," says the spaniel's owner as she sees me hesitate. I put Ms. Kitty down to see how she'll react. She handles dogs in one of two ways: either she arches her back in an arc that would make any yoga practitioner jealous, or she does what she is doing now—rolls over and waits for the dog to approach and rub her belly.

While the animals are socializing, I sit down at the picnic table and pull out the Asiago Chipotle Cheese sandwich I picked up from my favorite health store on the way out of town.

"Yum," says the woman, "that looks delicious. I didn't have time to prepare food so I ended up at the Roy Rogers." Her lip curls as she removes the burger gingerly from its paper wrapper. "Bad idea." She smiles. I try not to stare at her, but I can't help noticing how soft and deep her large brown eyes are, and the way her shiny, black hair sweeps across her forehead.

"What are you reading?" I ask.

"Portia de Rossi's memoir. I know it's been out

for ages, but I never got around to it."

Dyke? My gaydar is pinging. "So many books, so little time."

"Exactly!"

"Where you headed?" I ask her.

She bites into her burger. "Asheville, North Carolina." Hmm. Definitely a sizeable lesbian community there.

"Business or pleasure?"

"Business. I'm interviewing for a new job."

"Wouldn't it be easier to fly there?"

"Sure. But I'm terrified of flying. I know it's crazy, and I do fly when I have to, but I had the time, so I just decided to drive. And you?"

"I'm headed to Gulfport, in Florida. Have you heard of it?"

She moves her head and I'm not sure if she's nodding yes, or shaking it, no.

"It's very popular with uh…women. Kinda like Provincetown or Amherst, you know?"

"I've heard of Provincetown—it's a seaside place isn't it? And Amherst…is there a university there?" Not a dyke then. Too bad.

I finish up my sandwich. "I better head out. Still a long drive until tonight's stop." I scoop up Ms. Kitty. "Nice talking with you."

❧❧❧❧

Back on the road, I play my favorite Melissa Etheridge album and put my foot on the gas. Too bad about the chick at the rest stop—she really had beautiful eyes. Not sure why my gaydar wasn't tuned in better. But then again, nothing about my lesbian self seems to be tuned in these days. Maybe I'm not really a lesbian after all? Maybe my attraction to my English teacher at age 14 and all the affairs I've had ever since, coupled with my burning passion for Women's Studies and Womyn's music left me closed to the idea that I could be straight?

Who am I kidding? I'm as queer as they come. Although talking of coming, that's a sore subject these last couple of years.

Carmen, who mapped out my route, thought I could make it to Fayetteville tonight, but five hours later, approaching Richmond Virginia, I decide to call it a day. I find a motel off the freeway, settle Ms. Kitty on the bed, then head out to look for a place to eat. Just down the road, I see the large neon sign for a Denny's and decide that's probably as good as it's going to get.

Barely five minutes after the waitress seats me, I am startled by a voice behind me asking, "May I join you?" It's the Molly Pitcher dog-walking straight-gal. Still, company's company.

"Sure," I say, "please do." We both sit for a few minutes perusing the menu.

"So," she says, "what takes you to Gulfport, Florida?"

I wonder how much to tell her.

"I need a change of scene. I'm fed up with everything from shoveling snow to scraping teeth. I want a new job and a new social scene."

"Why there?"

"I—it sounds like the community might suit me."

"You're an artist? How exciting!" I look at her questioningly. I have no idea how she's made this assumption. "After we bumped into each other, I googled Gulfport," she says, noticing my puzzled expression. "It says it's a thriving artists' colony, with painters, sculptors, glassblowers, woodworkers..."

I decide it's time to take the spotlight off me. "Tell me about you. What's the job interview?"

"Gardens Crew Leader at the Biltmore Estate."

The Biltmore Estate? I've drooled over pictures on the internet. There's a gorgeous looking historical house, family home of the Vanderbilts, surrounded by thousands of acres of gardens. I wanted to stop and see it on my way down to Florida, but with Ms. Kitty and a carful of stuff, it didn't seem practical.

"Does that make you a landscaper? Gardener? Manager?"

She laughs. "All three. That's why I'm so excited about this new position."

"I'll bet. Must be a dream come true. The only place I know that sounds similar is Longwood Gardens in Delaware. Do you know it?"

"Know it? It's my favorite place to hang out!" I feel goosebumps on my arms. Isn't that exactly what I wrote on my dating profile? Too bad the bitch is straight.

"How likely are you to get the position?"

"It's mine if I want it. I've already had two skype interviews. They're ready to give me the job, but said I couldn't have it until I'd visited the grounds, met with the staff, and seen for myself that it's definitely where I want to be. But I do, I know I do." Her gorgeous brown eyes light up just talking about the job and for a moment I feel a stab of jealousy. I wish I felt that passionately about my own career. I can only hope Gulfport library will excite me as much as the grand house excites her, but as Carmen pointed out, and I refused to acknowledge, they may not even have any job openings, and even if they do, they might not be willing to hire a dental technician to hand out books to literary lesbians.

"You ladies ready to order?" The young girl who's asking looks all of sixteen. She's got long, dyed black hair, an earring in her nostril, and I'm pretty sure I spot a tattoo of a rainbow beneath her overall.

"Cool tatt." I look up at her and wink.

"Thanks." She flashes a smile. "My girlfriend and I got matching ones the day after our high school graduation." The girl readies her pen and looks to each of us, not sure who to ask first. "What'll it be?"

"I'll take the Veggie Skillet," we both say at exactly the same time, then laugh.

"And Tiffany thinks *I'm* co-dependent. At least we order different food when we go out. How long you two been together?"

"Oh…" I feel heat creeping up my neck to my cheeks which I know are bright red. "We're not—"

"Half an hour." Is she just being literal, or does she know what Tatt-girl was asking us? After the waitress leaves, I give her a questioning look.

"Okay, I'll come clean. I was just giving you a hard time. I know about P-town, and Gulfport, and what "community" means. I just had to test you a little."

"Test me?"

"The moment you walked over to the picnic table at Molly Pitcher, I had this absolute flash. Call me intuitive, but I just knew you were The One. Your aura was glowing, your face was open, and as for your body—you looked like a plump goddess." Plump is a word I can relate to. Goddess, not so much. I'm flabbergasted by what she said and reeling from the phrase she used: The One.

"I decided that if it was meant to be, somehow we'd meet up again. So I let you leave the rest area without asking you for any information. And then I walked into Denny's and here you are! So now I know for sure."

My stomach is churning so badly I'll never be able to touch that Veggie Skillet.

"So now what?" I whisper.

"Here's what I figure: Given what we've told each other about our current situations, we're going to have a long-distance relationship for a couple of years before you realize that you want to be with me forever. At that point you'll chuck in your job at the amazing library in Gulfport and join me at the Biltmore. Or, just possibly I'll resign from the Biltmore and come join you in Florida. Either way, in two years we're going to get married. I'm not sure whether we'll have kids; there are some things even I can't predict."

She leans across the table and grabs my face in her hands, pulling me so that our mouths meet and our tongues taste each other for the first time. My head is spinning, my stomach is flipping, and my body is on fire.

❧ ❧ ❧ ❧

She's wrong though. Because when you meet The One, there's no way you're going to jeopardize your relationship by making it long-distance. I never did get to Gulfport that year nor for a long time after. I went back to school and qualified as a psychologist so that I could finally understand why people who know flossing is good for them don't do it.

The first year of our retirement, we bought a twenty-four-foot camper and decided to head south to the Florida Keys for the winter.

࿇ ࿇ ࿇ ࿇

"There's somewhere I'd like to stop on the way," I tell her.

She thinks it's the Everglades, but I tell her no, it's on the other coast.

When she sees the freeway sign announcing that the next turnoff is Gulfport, a smile starts to play on her lips.

The first place we stop is the library. A shiny bronze plaque announces the dedication of the new building in 2045, thirty years to the day that gay marriage became legal in Florida. The plaque says that the library was dedicated by no less than President Malia Obama and her wife, Daniella Rubio. I lean on my walker and caress Cassie's silver hair.

"Thanks for indulging me," I tell her.

"Haven't I been doing that for the last twenty-nine years?"

I nod. She comes around my walker, pulls me toward her, and plants a kiss on my lips.

I feel light-headed, my stomach flips a little, and my body is filled with the warmth of a flame that's never going to be extinguished.

Alison grew up in England and lived in Israel and Mexico before settling in the USA. Her debut novel, *Along Came the Rain*, was published by Sapphire Books in April 2016. She loves doing puzzles, playing tennis and traveling with her wife Carol and their two rescue dogs.

Until Then

By Tara Wentz

Damn, what a morning," Tobi complained. Running her hands through her hair, she leaned back in her chair and closed her eyes for a moment. A brief smile claimed her lips as she thought back to just a few hours before she left the house to come to work.

"Ugh, I am so tired of taking it easy. C'mon, Tobi, give me my keys so I can go check on things at the apartment and run some errands."

"Ryan, I will give you your keys, but promise me you won't go alone. Have your Mom go with you."

"Honey, I am perfectly capable of doing things by myself now."

Tobi bit her lip and then nodded. "I know, I'd just feel better if Grace were there with you, just in case."

"You are exasperating, you know that don't you?" Ryan sighed before continuing. "Fine, I'll see if Mom has some time to go with me."

Tobi stepped closer and wrapped her arms around Ryan's waist. "Thank you, honey."

Ryan pulled Tobi closer and kissed her lips. "Ahuh, you know I can't deny you anything."

Tobi blushed and returned the kiss. "Well, I

wouldn't say *anything*, but hopefully soon," she ended with a wink.

Ryan grinned and leaned closer. "You promise?"

Tobi shivered and shook her head. Daydreaming wasn't going to get the work done. *Let's get this done so I can get home.* She was just about to start reading again when there was a knock on the door.

"Come in."

Marcy poked her head in and raised an eyebrow. "You got a second?"

Tobi turned in her chair and regarded Marcy. "Sure, what's up?"

Marcy stepped further into the room and leaned a hip against the desk. She worked with all the radiologists in the office, but Tobi was by far her favorite. "You remember that race car driver that broke her arm, Kellen Reynolds?"

"Yeah, sure. What about her?"

"Well, she's here and just wanted to know if you had a minute to go over the x-rays with her."

"Absolutely. Give me a few minutes to get the images pulled up and look over the reports. Show her in then, okay?"

"Gotcha, boss."

Tobi pulled up the images and finished reading the report as Marcy knocked again and opened the door.

Tobi stood with one hand outstretched. "Hi, I'm Dr. Tobi Drexler, nice to meet you."

"Hi, thank you so much for seeing us, Dr. Drexler," Kellen responded, shaking the proffered hand.

"Please, just call me Tobi. Have a seat," she indicated the chairs behind them.

Tobi waited while the woman and another lady had a seat in front of her desk.

"This is my partner, Joshlyn," Kellen introduced.

"Nice to meet you, Joshlyn. It's no problem at all. So, I know you are here to discuss the x-rays. Is there anything in particular that you want to know?"

While Tobi waited for the woman to answer she studied her and her partner. They were a very striking couple. Joshlyn's eyes were almost intimidating if not for the small laugh lines around them. The color was mesmerizing. She watched as Kellen's lips turned inward for a moment before she responded.

"I guess what I really want to know is how sturdy this arm is going to be. I need to be able to use both arms equally to drive."

"Ms. Reynolds—," she started.

"Kellen, please."

"Okay, Kellen. There is no reason to believe your arm won't be just as strong as it was before, maybe even stronger since you are doing physical therapy on it. The bones have healed quite nicely. Here, come closer and take a look."

Tobi turned towards the computer and showed them the before and after images. She also pointed out the fracture and the area of healing around it.

"I would not anticipate you having any issues."

Kellen's body relaxed and her features seemed less tense. "Great. That's...yeah, great news."

Tobi dipped her head in acknowledgement and regarded Joshyln. "Did you have any questions Joshlyn?"

"Not at all, Dr...er, Tobi. It's not easy watching her struggle with this. She's normally so sure focted and vibrant."

"Oh, believe me, I completely understand. I've got one of those at home myself."

Joshlyn laughed and nodded. "It's not fun. I'd rather be the one hurt."

"Right? Ryan can be a handful, but I wouldn't change her for the world."

"Hey, I'm right here you two!"

"Sorry, Kellen," Tobi grinned. "Things will be just fine. Finish the physical therapy and I guarantee you'll see what I'm talking about."

Kellen stood and reached a hand out. "Thanks, Doc. I appreciate everything."

Tobi walked them to the door and down the hall to the main waiting area. She stopped briefly in her steps when she spotted Ryan sitting and thumbing through a magazine. The blue-gray eyes peeked at her and then winked.

"You are more than welcome, Kellen." She stopped in front of her. "Ladies, this is my partner, Ryan Thomas. Ryan, this is Kellen and Joshlyn."

Ryan stood and shook both hands. "Kellen.. Kellen Reynolds, right?"

Kellen seemed momentarily shocked. "That's right."

"Yeah, I saw the highlights on the news a little while back on that big race you won. That was pretty spectacular."

Kellen blushed and ducked her head a little. "Thank you."

Tobi placed a hand on Ryan's arm. "That was a pretty incredible race."

"Are you fans of racing?"

"Well, actually, I've never been to a race, but it seems like it would be a lot of fun," Tobi answered and then glanced at Ryan.

"I've not been either, but I enjoy watching them."

"You guys will have to come to a race then. I'll get you tickets and you can come hang out with Josh in the pit," Kellen stopped abruptly. "If you want, that is, you know."

Joshlyn grinned. "It would be a blast. You guys should totally do it."

Tobi checked with Ryan, knowing full well she'd be more than happy to go. Seeing her nod, she looked back to Kellen.

"You know, that sounds like a lot of fun." She grabbed one of her cards and wrote her number on it. "Here's my cell number. Give me a call when you guys are ready to do this and we'll be there."

They all shook hands and promised to get together in the near future.

⁂

Ryan waited as Tobi showed Kellen and Joshlyn the rest of the way out and smiled as she turned back around to make her way to Ryan's side.

"Aren't you a sight for sore eyes?" Tobi asked, leaning in for a hug.

"I was a good girl and did as you asked. Mom went with me and we checked on the apartment. I just dropped her off and thought maybe you'd have time for some lunch." Ryan held up the bag of food.

"Oh, that sounds wonderful. Marcy, I'm going to grab a quick bite with Ryan. Can you hold my calls, please?"

"You got it, boss."

Tobi rolled her eyes and pulled Ryan down the

hall.

Once they were seated Ryan pulled the sandwiches out and handed one to Tobi. They ate in silence for a bit before Ryan spoke up.

"So, Kellen Reynolds, huh?" She asked taking a big bite of her sandwich.

"Yep. Who knew she was so damn attractive?"

Ryan chewed, swallowed and then laughed. "I think you just have a thing for brunettes with long hair."

"Well, I cannot lie. However, there is only one…" she set the last bit of her sandwich down and stood, "long-haired brunette…" she walked around the desk towards Ryan, "that I am interested in, and…" she sat right in Ryan's lap, "that's you, my love." She leaned in and took Ryan's lips with her own.

Ryan grasped Tobi's hips and jerked her closer. She bit down on Tobi's bottom lip, forcing a startled gasp out of her. Releasing the lip, she traced it lightly with her tongue. She took her mouth again in a long sinful tangle that immediately made her wet between the thighs. One hand found the buttons on Tobi's blouse and one by one they came loose. Ryan brought a sensual onslaught to Tobi's neck and nipped gently before dragging her lips up to a small ear.

"You are so damn beautiful, Tobi. You take my breath away," she whispered.

Tobi seemed incapable of words as Ryan again took her lips in a crushing kiss.

Ryan's hand made it inside Tobi's shirt and beneath the cup of her bra. She rubbed lightly across the turgid nipple before squeezing it between her fingertips.

"Oh!" Tobi gasped.

"Mmm, I love this about you, sweetheart. You are so responsive."

Ryan lowered her head and pushed the bra aside. She traced around the hardened nipple with her tongue before sucking it into her mouth. Tobi's heart thudded erratically against Ryan's cheek. She continued teasing her nipple and breast and brought her free hand down to Tobi's thigh. She raked her fingernails up and down her thigh until Tobi started squirming on her lap. She slid her hand underneath Tobi's skirt and squeezed her thigh firmly.

"Tobi, honey, we are almost past the point of no return. Now is your chance to tell me to stop."

"Don't you dare stop," Tobi rasped.

Ryan chuckled and slid her hand all the way up under the skirt and against the front of Tobi's panties.

"You are so incredibly wet, my love and I am so glad you are not wearing hose today."

"Ryan, please don't take this the wrong way, but shut up," Tobi begged.

Ryan couldn't keep the smile from her face. She kissed those pouty lips and brought her nose down to the soft skin of Tobi's neck. She inhaled deeply and at the same time slid her hand inside the legging on her panties. Fingers grazed across the most sensitive parts before gliding their way into the wet folds. Slowly her hand progressed and just as her fingers plunged deep inside Tobi, she bit down on her neck.

Tobi cleaved onto Ryan, begging her not to stop. "Please, please, just do it, Ryan. I need you so much."

Ryan set a steady pace and slipped a thumb out to rub against her clit. A fine sheen of sweat covered Tobi's face and the valley between her breasts. Ryan rubbed her cheek against the base of her throat. The muscles were taught and her breathing was erratic. It wouldn't take much more to send her over the edge.

"Let it go, baby."

"So good, Ryan. So, so good."

"That's it, let me hear you."

"Ryan, I'm…oh—,"

Tobi's body contracted as the orgasm hit her. She gasped but held her voice.

"Oh honey, you are so amazing." Ryan held her while the aftershocks shook her body. Slowly she regained her equilibrium, but still sat clinging to Ryan.

"You ambushed me, Thomas."

Ryan detected not even a hint of anger in that statement. Deep down both of them had been missing the intimacy. The recovery time for Ryan's shooting put a huge damper on things, but not anymore. As of this morning she was completely cleared to proceed with any activities she desired. Tobi was definitely something she desired…but more importantly needed. Vincent, Tobi's stalker, was not going to be an issue. He'd been shot and killed after holding Ryan hostage and shooting her in front of Tobi. They were now free to resume life and their relationship. She gave Tobi a peck on the lips, helped her straighten her clothes and then waited for her to stand.

Tobi stood and held a hand out to Ryan. "You were a definite welcome surprise. Thank you so much for the lunch, but even more for…well, you know."

The blush across Tobi's cheeks made Ryan's heart skip a beat. She was sure she'd never be able to live without this woman and couldn't wait to get their lives started.

"Just thought I'd give you something to think about until you get home tonight." Ryan walked to the door with a smug grin on her face, never breaking eye contact with Tobi.

Tobi grinned back. "Until then."

Tara lives in Missouri with her partner and has been in the medical field for over 25 years. When not working or writing, Tara likes to read, dabble with photography and watch sports. She has two novels, Traffic Stop and Deception by Design, and is currently at work on her third.

What A Pair

By Lorraine Howell

I waited at the airport with heart pounding, palms sweaty and brain working overtime. My youngest son was due to arrive from Los Angeles at any moment. I was beyond happy and a little bit nervous. I was going to officially "come out" to him and though I figured he already knew that I was a lesbian since I have been living with Sweetie for over a year and a half, I wanted to make it official. Besides, Sweetie does not like sleeping alone and I figured that once I crawled in bed beside her it would be a dead giveaway. I had decided to come out to my youngest first since he is my open-minded, model/actor son. Those that live in La-La Land tend to be more understanding. I knew he would not judge us or go bat shit crazy or threaten to jump off a bridge. My daughter is the emotional bridge-jumper and she is up next for the big unveiling. Can't wait for that one. Oh yay! Then comes the Baptist youth minister son with many opinions that he is always willing to share. Yeesh! Now can you understand why I wanted to begin with the youngest? I thought so.

I saw him as he walked out the door at the airport and jumped into the front seat beside me. His copper red hair gleamed. His light blue eyes sparkled.

He was just beautiful. I had missed him more than I even realized. I decided then to wait a day to tell him so that we could just talk and enjoy each other. Sweetie would understand and give me one night out of our bed…maybe. The talk flowed easily as I asked him about his flight, his auditions, his girlfriend, his life in general. We went to his favorite rib shack and ate some lunch then we headed home. On the way, I started to sweat again. I had not "de-dyked" the house. There were pictures of me and Sweetie out on the table as you walked in the door. It was fairly obvious that only the dogs slept in the guest room due to the large amounts and varying colors of hair on the sheets. Our lesbian romance novels filled the living room shelves. My night clothes were laying on the foot of OUR bed. I had to tell him. It could not wait. I needed a valium. Or a drink. Or both. Both sounded really good about now.

We arrived at home, he grabbed his suitcase and in we went. He was mauled by the dogs first. He loved it. He sat in the middle of them and let them lick him to death while he laughed joyously. I kept peeking at the picture of me and Sweetie sitting on the shelf right by his shoulder. Gulp. Could I slip around and lay the picture on its front? Should I? Before I could make up my mind, he got up and began walking around the house looking at everything. He loved the house and commented on paint color, the built-ins, the homey feel of the place. This was his first visit and he had to see, taste, and touch everything. He is a curious and tactile boy. He gets that from me.

He touched the picture of me and Sweetie and said, "Oh this is a good picture of you and Sweetie. Ya'll look happy."

An opening. Yes. Here was my chance. "Thank

you,"I gulped. Then I froze up. My throat refused to allow another word to escape. Damn. Opportunity lost.

I showed him to his room. He loved the remodeling that we had done in there. Sweat was dripping off of my nose and from underneath my boobs. I also felt it begin to run down my butt-crack. I was in total melt-down. We walked back into the living room and sat down on the sofa. Talk flowed freely again. He told me all about his Improv group and the show that they had just put on. He laughed about one of the games that they had performed where he had to be angry and just blurt out sayings randomly. For some reason, all he could think to say was "Fuck You." Loudly. Very loudly! I was so proud. He continued telling me about the show and I continued to sweat and shake and wonder when to just spit my news out.

"Can you see everyone's faces mom? Other actors were saying things like "look the flowers are blooming in such lovely colors," and I yelled, "Fuck you" at them. No matter what they said, I just screamed "Fuck you." Everyone was shocked since that is so out of character for me and they had to try not to crack up which just made it more fun for me. "Fuck you," "Fuck you," "Fuck you." He was getting louder and louder and laughing harder and harder.

"Sweetie and I are a couple," I spat out.

"Fuck you," he shouted laughing, still caught up in the game.

"No really. We are a couple. Like a real couple. You know the kind that sleeps together and has se… ummm…everything that comes with being a real pair," I blurted out in a rush.

Silence. Fear washed over me.

"She is really, really good to me and she loves me

and I love her and we have made a home together…"
I continued.

More silence. The sweat started to drip harder.
It was like a faucet was attached to the end of my nose
and the boob sweat was now running into my shorts
commingling with my butt-crack sweat.

"I am happy son. Really happy."

Nothing.

"Say something. Please. Anything. I can take it,"
I implored.

Then I detected the sweat on his face. Noticed
the trembling of his hands. Saw the complete look of
fear in his eyes.

"Son, what is wrong? Do you hate me? Are you
shocked? Grossed out? What? Talk to momma please,"
I begged.

Again I was met with silence. This boy is never
quiet. Never at a loss for words. Had I really shocked
him? Did he hate me?

"Speak to me baby. I am still your momma. Tell
me what you think."

Finally he looked me right in the eyes and said,
"I love you momma. I could never hate you. I think it
is great that you and Sweetie are together and happy.
You smile a lot and that means so much to me. I could
never be shocked or grossed out. I am engaged. You
are happy. That is wonderful. I am glad you found
someone."

What a wonderful, understanding son. He loves
me and accepts me and is happy for us. He is engaged.
He is not gross…huh? He is engaged? Excuse me!

"Thank you son for understanding. I love you
so much. Ummmm, did you say you are engaged or
enraged," I asked.

"I am engaged momma. I love her so much. I know that we are young and are trying to get established in our careers but we will have a long engagement and we are smart and know that we have to get everything together before we actually marry and…" Now he was rambling.

I was silent.

"Oh momma, please be happy for me, for us. I thought it through. I even bought her a beautiful ring. She is very important to me," he continued.

My throat was dry. This was my baby. What did I feel? How should I handle this? Boy had the conversation gone in a different direction than I had expected.

"I am happy momma. She makes me happy. Just like Sweetie makes you happy. Can you understand that? Please. For me."

He looked just like he did when he was six years old. He wanted my approval. He needed my approval, much as I had wanted and needed his. We were in the same boat. We were two scared individuals that loved each other desperately and wanted happiness each for the other.

More silence. I was shocked. I knew that it showed on my face. I growled at him vociferously. The same growl that I used to scare him with when he was a child.

The look on his face was priceless. He looked like I was going to cut his wee-wee off. I burst into laughter. We were both big ole chickens that had kept something very important from one another due to fear. How silly we were. He started laughing too.

"Wow, what a pair we are huh, Ma? We were absolutely making ourselves crazy because we were afraid how the other would react. We are family. Family accepts each other. No matter what. I love you momma. You could do nothing to make me hate you. You are my bestest friend in the whole world," he was still giggling like a little school girl.

"So, have you told your brother yet," I asked.

"Have you," he replied.

"Not a chance," I said.

"Hell Naw, me neither," he chuckled.

"So, we are ok now huh," I asked.

"Well, yea, DUH," he replied. "But I do have one question for you."

"Shoot," I replied.

"How do you guys 'do it?'" he asked with a wicked grin.

"Fuck you," I hooted hysterically as we hugged.

Lorraine Howell lives in South Florida with her Sweetie and their 3 dogs. A yappy, overweight min-pin with an attitude named Juno, a very fluffy long-haired German Shepherd sweetheart named Cricket and the newest member of the family, Bubba from da'Glades, a mixed breed rescue puppy with some strange fears (grass anyone?). Lorraine is working on the sequel to The Happy Lesbian Housewife - You Can't Make This Stuff Up. Seriously!

A Place on the Wall

By Kayt C. Peck

The Commander's hand shook as she poured coffee into a chipped and stained cup. That cup had been her companion for more years than most of her friends. The liquid was hot and strong, like the coffee on which she depended during the long hours of the night watch aboard the USS Mercy...like the coffee that was a taste of home when surrounded by the steamy tropics of Vietnam. Day or night, there was always coffee waiting as she sought refuge in the mess tent of the Combat Zone Fleet Hospital that was her first tour of duty. She saw death daily, and because of that, the taste of coffee came to mean more. It was as though she must continue to enjoy the simple pleasure now denied the men she could no longer help, could not have saved.

The Commander sat alone at a table, enjoying, as best she could, what was quiet possibly her millionth cup of Navy coffee. It was likely to be her last.

A slight breeze stirred the room as the door to the crew's lounge peeked open. Corpsman Slater stuck his head through the open doorway. Laugh lines surrounded his now sober eyes, and the Commander smiled at the familiar face. For two years she'd been unit commanding officer. For two years, she watched this sensitive, good-natured man serve as his shipmates' healer. For two years she'd heard the laughter he elicited in his co-workers. Today, there was no laughter. The gregarious sailor was subdued in manner and speech.

"Commander, can we come in?" the veteran asked.

"Of course, Slater. What a question . . . this is the crew's lounge, you know."

The door opened, and Slater led a file of his shipmates from CBTZ 22 Detachment 1410. The Commander felt a wash of pride as, one by one, almost all of the twenty-three members of the medical unit filed through the door. No one spoke. They sat around the tables, on the couch and atop the edge of the pool table. Soon, there was nowhere to sit. That didn't stop them. They leaned against the walls or along the counter. Anywhere they could find a spot, they were there, all of them . . . all but one.

Her gaze darted around the room, looking for the telltale color of khaki, searching for the man who was her right-hand. Where's the Chief, she wondered.

"He wanted to be here, but he couldn't," Slater said, answering her unspoken question.

"Yes, I'd forgotten," the Commander responded. "He can't see me until after he testifies."

The Commander forgot the absence of her executive officer as she looked around the room. How many times had she looked at those same faces . . . in the classroom, standing in ranks, working side-by-side, covered in sweat and dirt during field exercises? In many ways, they were her family. Her heart contracted with a wave of love and grief. As she looked into the familiar faces of her people, she saw a reflection of those same emotions.

The Commander shook her head and willed her face into a smile.

"It's not the end of the world, folks," she said.

"It damn sure feels like it," said Garcia from his spot at the back of the room. The Commander was surprised. Garcia had always been distant, a little uncomfortable with a female as his superior officer. Earning his respect was difficult.

"Come on, Slater," the Commander prompted. "Tell us a joke."

Slater looked at the woman who had been his leader. His gaze was soft and deep. "I thought I could always find something funny." He smiled without amusement. "I guess I was wrong."

The Commander felt a brushing touch against her hand. She turned to look into the tear-filled eyes of Hospitalman Apprentice Guthrie. The girl, still a child in the Commander's eyes, was both the newest and the youngest member of the unit. Sometimes the Commander wondered how the delicate creature survived boot camp. The Commander had taken special care, not to protect the girl, but to help her build the confidence that would carry her through life. The child was not as delicate as she seemed, and the Commander was pleased to see the fledgling development of a capable young woman.

"Did you have to tell them?" the girl said. She took a deep breath, fighting back tears.

The gentleness stayed in the Commander's eyes, but her mouth became hard and set. "Yes, Guthrie. I had to tell them. It was time."

"Ma'am, we don't want to lose you," another corpsman said.

The Commander looked around the room, her

gaze touching every face. "And I don't want to lose you."

All eyes turned to the door as it opened abruptly. Captain William Harmon paused, an old and nasty coffee cup in his hand. He looked surprised as he took in the room, pausing for an instant before crossing authoritatively toward the coffee pot.

The Commander looked at her hands, unsure what to say. Captain Harmon was an old friend. He was also chairman of the administrative review board who now held her Naval career in the balance. She knew he would do his job, despite the friendship, and she would respect him nonetheless. She said nothing, for it would be improper to speak.

There was a stern set to his jaw as the veteran officer poured his coffee. Abruptly, he set the half-filled cup on the counter, splashing coffee on the Navy-clean surface.

"Damn it, Liz," he said as he turned to face the Commander. He looked around the room, took a deep breath and decided to gamble his career. "All you got to do is deny it. Say you're not a lesbian, and I'll see it ends here. As far as I'm concerned it's nobody's God-damned business who you sleep with anyway. Why make this sacrifice?"

The room went perfectly still. No one dared breathe as they waited for the Commander's answer. She sat and looked into the blackness of her coffee, and the silence grew. When she finally spoke, her voice was soft, but no one failed to hear.

"A couple of months ago, I finally went to the Vietnam Memorial," she said.

"What the Hell has that got to do with this?" Harmon demanded.

The Commander stood and her eyes stared into emptiness, seeing not the room before her, the beloved faces of her people, but a cold, black marble wall. They all watched as she raised her hand, still staring at the monument that was there but not there. They saw her fingers move, tracing the outlines of a name etched in black marble.

"Jane Aston Taylor," she said. Her hand dropped to her side. "She was a lieutenant, junior grade when I was at Fleet Hospital 12 in Vietnam." The Commander's eyes filled with tears and all present knew that she was looking into the past. "She was my first true love."

"Liz, if you tell me this, I'll have to …"

"We shared a tent with three other nurses, and we shared Hell with everyone in the outfit. Death and destruction paraded through our lives on a daily basis, and so we all learned how to live. We learned to see what was important and ignore the surface shit." The Commander looked directly into Captain Harmon's eyes. "I felt no shame when I realized my love for a strong and gentle woman who could laugh and cry with equal abandon. I felt no shame when that love naturally turned to a physical intimacy. The other nurses in our tent knew, and they didn't care. One of them told me that it was such a relief to see love, any love in the midst of all that death."

The Commander swished the now-cold coffee in her cup before she continued. "They left us alone when they could. The other three would take leave together or volunteer for shifts together, leaving Jane and me to ourselves. I often wondered how awkward it must feel for the other women to have to knock at the door of their own quarters, but they did, and they never complained, teased and laughed but never complained.

"We were alone when the final call came," tears spilled down the Commander's cheeks. "We were alone just before she died." The Commander took a ragged breath and continued. "No major combat action was anticipated, and our three tent-mates had finagled passes. It was the second night, and Jane and I slept with complete abandon, wrapped in each other's arms. A knock came to the door, it was the company *Personnelman*. A call had come from one of the emergency stations. There had been an accident and they needed a nurse to assist the doctor. I had the late shift the night before, so Jane pushed me back on the bunk, calling that she would take the call. Sleep was almost as precious as love in those days, and I barely woke to mumble for her to be safe. She gently kissed me goodbye before pulling on her uniform and heading out the door.

"The Petty Officer was driving when they hit the mine. His right foot was nearly severed when the explosion came through the floor. He said Jane looked in good shape. She had taken some shrapnel, but she was mobile, and had placed a tourniquet on his badly bleeding leg before she started having trouble breathing. You see, a hunk of metal, most likely from the Jeep, had pierced her right lung."

It did not seem possible, but the silence in the room grew even more intense. The Commander cried, but not alone.

"Jane died by the side of the road, drowned in her blood. The Petty Officer said she died with her hands still tying the dressing on his leg." The Commander shook visibly, emotion running through her entire body. "The Petty Officer told me her final words were, 'Tell Liz, I love her, and I always will.'"

No one spoke. No one moved. The Commander's sobs were the only sound. Guthrie placed her hand inside the Commander's. The older woman grasped at the welcomed comfort. After a few moments, the Commander straightened, regaining the dignity for which they all knew her. She turned to face Captain Harmon.

"Respectfully, sir, I will no longer deny my sexuality, and I will no longer deny what I shared with Jane Taylor."

Captain Harmon picked up his half-forgotten coffee. "I can't re-write the law, Liz."

"I know, sir, and I know you've got to do what you've got to do."

The Captain left the room abruptly, hiding the tears that filled his own eyes.

Love and respect hung in the air like a scent. Her people watched as the Commander sat, still gathering her dignity. Slater stood and walked to the coffee pot. He filled the Commander's cup with her last taste of Navy coffee.

THE END

Kayt Peck draws on a rich life experience in her fiction. Whether reviving life in the Navy, on the ranch, or in the labyrinth of relationship, she strives to give her stories a flavor of truth. Her novels, Good Water and The Ladies Room reflect that core of truth.

Other Anthology by Sapphire Books Authors

The One: Stories of Falling in Love Forever - ISBN - 978-1-943353-32-3

If lucky enough, we fall in love once in a lifetime.

Children's books and romance novels promise us an encounter with a beautiful, mythical love – a passionate lover that sweeps us off kilter and changes everyday life into happily-ever-after. In reality, most fall in love a couple of times throughout a lifetime. Yet, those relationships fail to fulfill the "forever" expectancy – they end. Still, we hope that love, true and eternal will embrace us. We hope that stardust will cover the banal when life becomes monotonous or loneliness grasps us too firmly when days fades to night.

Reading about love triumphant sparks desire for more than uninspired routine existence.

In The One, an assortment of writers chronicle the discovery of the one woman to share the rest of life's journey.

Everyone deserves happily ever after!